The Guardian Angel

Bridget Essex

Rose + Star Press

The Guardian Angel

Books by Bridget Essex

A Wolf for Valentine's Day
A Wolf for the Holidays
Don't Say Goodbye
Forever and a Knight
A Knight to Remember
Wolf Town
Dark Angel
Big, Bad Wolf
The Protector (Lone Wolf, Book 1)
Meeting Eternity: The Sullivan Vampires, Vol. 1

With Natalie Vivien

The Vampire Next Door

The Guardian Angel

About the Author

My name is Bridget Essex, and I've been writing about vampires for almost two decades. I'm influenced most by classic vampires– the vision of CARMILLA (it's one of the oldest lesbian novels!) and DRACULA. My vampires have always been kind of traditional (powerful), but with the added self-torture of regret and the human touch of guilt.

I have a vast collection of knitting needles and teacups, and like to listen to classical music when I write. My first date with my wife was strolling in a garden, so it's safe to say I'm a bit old fashioned. I have a black cat I love very much, and a brown dog who actually convinces me to go outside. When I'm actually outside, I begin to realize that writing isn't all there is to life. Just most of it! I'm married to the love of my life, author Natalie Vivien.

The love story of the beautiful but tragic vampire Kane Sullivan and her sweetheart Rose Clyde is my magnum opus, and I'm thrilled to share it with you in ***The Sullivan Vampires*** series, published by **Rose and Star Press**! Find out more at **www.LesbianRomance.org** and **http://BridgetEssex.Wordpress.com**

The Guardian Angel
Copyright © 2015 Bridget Essex - All Rights Reserved
Published by Rose and Star Press
First edition, May 2015

This is a work of fiction. Names, characters, places and incidents either are products of the author's imagination or are used fictitiously. Any resemblance to actual events or locales or persons, living or dead, is entirely coincidental.

This book, or parts thereof, may not be reproduced without written permission.

ISBN: 1511735570
ISBN-13: 978-1511735575

The Guardian Angel

The Guardian Angel

DEDICATION

For my angel, Natalie.

The Guardian Angel

Chapter 1: The No Good, Very Bad Day

I smile at the camera with my best fake smile as Scott, my camera guy, counts me in to the live broadcast. I lift the microphone to my mouth, straighten my back and stand as tall as I can, chin up.

Hey, this may be the *stupidest* story I've ever reported on...but I can still be professional about it, right?

In the background, a whoopee cushion goes off and yet another whipped cream pie sails past my head, missing me by a fraction of an inch. I sigh for a long moment.

"Three," mouths Scott, "two...one..."

I take a deep breath and smile even wider as I begin: "This is Erin McEvoy with BEAN, reporting on the..." I try not to grimace and think I manage to contort my mouth into a playful sideways smile, but Scott is sawing his thumb back and forth across his neck and shaking his head. My lips go slack, and I swallow. "Reporting on the whipped cream pie fight that broke out due to a disagreement between two clowns at the Clowning Around

Convention, taking place in downtown Boston today."

There. I got through the introduction without a) laughing hysterically or b) rolling my eyes. This means that my report is off to a *great* start, all things considered.

"Behind me," I say, gesturing toward the melee of brightly colored clowns wielding tins of whipped cream, "the pie fight goes on, a battle that began more than a quarter of an hour ago..."

One of the clowns nearby yells out an expletive, but I clear my throat and keep talking. Hey, it's live TV—and video of a clown shouting profanity might go viral. "According to witnesses, the disagreement started between Bumbo the clown and Bilbo the clown," I tell the camera, hoping that my smile doesn't look *quite* as strained as it feels. "They smashed pie plates full of whipped cream—made up for an Art of the Pie Smash demonstration—in each other's faces, but then their friends joined in, and soon the entire convention hall was covered in sticky whipped cream."

Another pie sails past my head, but I don't even flinch.

"The Clowning Around Convention has now been postponed due to unsafe—or, rather, slippery—conditions. Doodle is a professional clown who works with both Bilbo and Bumbo and has the inside scoop," I say, clearing my throat and turning to my left, where Doodle, a woman dressed in polka-dotted suspenders, wearing a giant red nose and a curly green wig, stands smiling. Well, the smile is painted onto her face.

"Doodle, can you give us your eyewitness account of the pie fight?"

But before the clown opens her mouth, a pie plate piled high with fluffy whipped cream flies through the air, making a beeline for my face...

I don't have time to react, to duck—even to blink. The pie hits me squarely, sliding down my nose and bouncing off my chest before clattering to the floor.

I sigh, keep smiling, because if I learned anything from my very first job, it's this: when it comes to live TV, the show must go on, *no matter what*.

"We seem to have gotten into a bit of a sticky situation ourselves here at the convention," I say, with enthusiasm. "This is Erin McEvoy for BEAN. Back to you in the studio, Dirk."

In my earpiece, I can already hear Dirk Dixon, lead anchor at BEAN, chuckling in his inherently smarmy way. "Thanks for the *sweet* story, Erin," he says, with maximum condescension, which makes me not-so-secretly fume. Scott cuts the live feed, lowers his camera and lifts his finger with a little shrug.

"I'll...uh...get you a paper towel?"

"That'd be lovely," I tell him, then wipe my hand over my face, holding my microphone out at arm's length so it doesn't get covered in the white goo.

"Sorry about that," says Doodle, the clown I didn't end up interviewing. I glance at her through a haze of whipped cream, and—surprisingly—she *does* look sorry. Or, at least, as sorry as someone *can* look when a gigantic red smile is makeupped onto her face.

I clear my throat again, shaking my head. "Hey, not your fault," I tell Doodle, trying to smile. "I'm sorry I didn't get a chance to interview you on air," I tell her, as Scott presses a paper towel into my hands. I think that was Scott, anyway. Whipped cream: super tasty to eat, surprisingly vision-impairing when smashed into your eyes.

After I wipe off my face and can sort of see again, I realize that Scott hasn't come back yet, and it was Doodle who handed me the paper towel.

"Anyway," says Doodle, her head tilted to one side. "It was really nice meeting you, Erin."

It's impossible to tell what Doodle the clown *actually* looks like under all that grease paint. There's too much of it, and it's expertly applied, covering her face in a nightmare-inducing mask. Maybe I watched *It* too many times when I was a kid. Clowns just...creep me out.

Still, Doodle seems nice enough. The only parts of her face that aren't concealed in makeup are her eyes. They're... Well, those have to be contact lenses, right? *No one* has *turquoise* eyes. They're bright and blue-green and...gorgeous.

Hey, it's been a rotten day. A clown's pretty turquoise eyes have been the only highlight, and I'm going to have to cling to that.

I guess things could be worse.

"Yeah, it was nice meeting you, too," I tell her, turning toward Scott as he runs up, a roll of paper towels in hand.

"What did you say?" he asks me, blinking.

"Oh, I was just talking to Doodle..." I turn to gesture toward the clown and blink.

Hmm. I didn't get *that* much whipped cream in my eyes. I saw Doodle here just a second ago. Half a second ago.

And now she's gone.

Like, *completely* gone. The whipped cream pies are still flying, and there are a handful of non-pie-throwing clowns milling around, but I don't think Doodle could have slipped away so quickly. The crowd is too thin.

"Well, that's weird," I mutter to myself, tearing off a handful of paper towels from the roll and toweling off my face with them. "We have a disappearing clown."

"It's probably part of her act. A

disappearing *magician* clown or something," says Scott with a shrug. "I found a bathroom if you want to wash up, Erin," he tells me, jerking his thumb over his shoulder.

I leave Scott to pack up the equipment as I soap-and-water my face in the convention center's bathroom. Then I wait for him in the station jeep. "BEAN" is detailed on the jeep doors in big, yellow letters, and the jeep itself is a vomit-colored green. While, admittedly, vomit-colored green is not my favorite color, we're a pretty small station and we have a pretty small budget, and the gross-colored mode of transportation means that I can find the jeep easily in a crowded parking lot.

Traditionally, I'm a glass half-full kind of gal. But even with my inherent optimism, I have to admit—today was a trial.

As I wait in the jeep, wondering if the smell of whipped cream will ever come out of my hair, my phone—hidden somewhere in the depths of my purse—makes the little chirping sound that tells me I just got a text message. I fish out my cell, wiping a bit of whipped cream off the side of my purse and licking my finger.

There's a text from Ginger, my best friend forever...who will probably never let me live down the fact that a pie was thrown in my face on live television. I'm guessing she just watched my report on TV.

The text opens up with, *So I'm thinking*

you won't want the pie I made for dessert?

I groan but then chuckle and thumb through the rest of the text. Ginger's asking if I'm still up to coming to her place for dinner tonight.

I put my chin in my hands and glance out the side window of the jeep with a sigh. Honestly? I want nothing more than to go home, take a long, hot bath, cuddle in bed with my collie, Sawyer (named after my idol, Diane Sawyer), and disappear into a romance novel.

But I've been blessed with a guilty conscience, and I don't want to disappoint Ginger.

After all, she made me a pie. Which, true, I probably won't be able to stomach, given the day's events. I shiver as a flashback of the whipped cream colliding with my face assaults me.

Still...

I'll be there in about an hour, Ginger—as long as I can skip the pie! I text her.

She texts me back instantly: *I was joking about the pie, you loon. I made you strawberry shortcake.*

And before I can reply to that one, she sends another text: *Wear something nice, okay?*

I stare at my phone and frown. We joke around, the two of us, but for some reason, I don't think that last text from Ginger was a joke.

Wear something nice? What the heck? I

always wear something nice. Unless...

I drop my phone back into my purse, my brow raised. She wouldn't. Ginger wouldn't do that to me. Not again.

She wouldn't set me up on a date. Would she?

"Hey, I'm sorry about today," says Scott with an apologetic smile, opening up the jeep's driver's side door and climbing in.

"Don't be," I tell him, grinning. I shrug. "It was an eye-opening day. And...eye-burning. If I get into another pie-fighting contest, let me tell you...I'm going to be prepared!"

"I wouldn't doubt that," says Scott mildly, casting me a sidelong smile. He puts the jeep into drive, and then we're peeling out of the convention center parking lot, and I'm rolling down the windows, letting the sweet summer air roll on into the jeep, blowing away the pervasive, too-sweet scent of whipped cream.

"Lulu came up with some pretty good new jokes last night," says Scott, turning onto the highway. Lulu is Scott's four-year-old daughter, and for a little kid, she is quite the comedian.

I could use some humor right now, and Scott knows it. "Lay 'em on me," I tell him, smiling.

"Knock-knock!" he sings.
"Who's there?"
"Cherry."

"Cherry who?"

"Cherry up!"

In spite of myself, I burst out laughing. "God, that's a groaner. But impressive for a four-year-old," I tell him, still chuckling.

"I've got more," he tells me with a wink. And then: "Knock-knock!"

"Who's there?" I ask, pulling my purse onto my lap. We're getting close to my apartment, and Scott—peach that he is—promised to drop me off early because of my dinner with Ginger.

"Maybe."

"Maybe who?"

"Maybe we should have a dance party!"

I smile and shake my head. "Unfortunately, my dancing days are over," I tell him, but Scott is laughing.

"Seriously? What are you, thirty? And your dancing days are *over*?"

"Well, technically, they never began. I'm an awful dancer." I grimace.

Scott says, brows up, "Well, maybe you just haven't met the right dance partner yet."

I chuckle, shaking my head again.

"No, I'm being serious! Look at me... I mean, I used to hate dancing, too—until Sylvia convinced me to take some classes."

Sylvia is Scott's amazing wife, who always sends him to work with an extra slice of cake for me whenever she's baked one of her secret family recipes. "Ballroom dancing?" I ask him incredulously.

He shakes his head, a mischievous smile on his boyish face. "Nope. Dirty."

I snort with laughter.

He holds up a hand, "Hey, Patrick Swayze I'm *not*, but I learned to stop worrying about making an idiot of myself. Valuable life lesson right there." He tips up his nose and winks meaningfully at me.

I groan, sink back into the passenger seat as I ponder my pie-in-the-face moment, *live on camera*, for the *entire city of Boston* to see—that is, if they ever bothered tuning in to our news station. Well, I've got that going in my favor, at least: very few people watch the BEAN.

I cradle my chin in my hand, glance out at the blue skies and puffy white clouds floating beyond the window.

Sure, I'd like to stop worrying about making an idiot out of myself... But that isn't a life lesson I've mastered quite yet.

⌛

"Thanks for dropping me off, Scott—I owe you one!" I tell him as he pulls up in front of my apartment building.

"Hey, I'm not the one who got clobbered by a clown today," he tells me with a warm smile. "You don't owe me anything."

"Tell Sylvia and Lulu that I said hello!" I say with a wave of my hand as I hop down out of the jeep.

I left my windows open today to the sweet breeze from the ocean washing down the street...and even though I live three stories up, dogs have *great* hearing. Sawyer sticks her adorable, pointy-nosed head out of the living room window, peers down at me with big, brown eyes and starts barking at me. Even her barks sound lazy.

Scott pulls away, and I trot up the three flights of stairs to my front door. Sawyer is sitting placidly on the other side, and when I get the door open, dropping the keys on the table by the door, she takes two steps forward, sniffs my proffered hand, and begins to lick it thoughtfully—like you might lick a new flavor of ice cream that you aren't sure you're going to enjoy.

"Thanks for that," I tell her with a laugh, tousling the fur behind her ears and clipping her leash to her collar.

It's official: my beautiful collie is as round as a beach ball and *really* needs more exercise than her current couch potato life affords her. I try to make it home halfway through the day to take her on a nice, long walk (for my benefit, just as much as for hers), but things keep coming up, crazy news stories break (and I *always* get the crazy ones), and then she doesn't get her three walks a day...

And Sawyer grows just a *little* bit rounder.

Take this evening, for example. If I don't walk her very quickly around the block, I'm not going to have enough time to take a shower before I show up at Ginger's. And I *need* to take a shower. I still feel sticky all over. Don't get me wrong—whipped cream is one of my favorite foods. To eat, though—not to wear.

So Sawyer and I take our speediest walk yet, while I promise her that that, this weekend, we're going to clock in a couple of miles on some beach trails. Sawyer glances at me placidly as if to say, "Yeah, right, Mom," and then we're back home, I'm unclipping her leash, and throwing myself headlong into the shower.

I get my hair wet, considering what I should wear tonight. My eyes are closed, the water sluicing over my face, and when I reach for the shampoo, it's in my hand and hair before the scent catches up with me.

And I freeze, the hot water pounding against my body.

"Well, crap," I mutter, the scent of Melinda's shampoo tickling my nose.

Melinda was my old girlfriend...which is still a really weird thing to say. My old girlfriend. The *ex*. We broke up two months ago, and I've been so busy with work that I just haven't gotten around to removing all the bits of

Melinda that still linger around my apartment. This weekend... This weekend I need to purge my home of all things Melinda-saturated.

Truthfully? I guess I've had time (my *Jeopardy!*-watching addiction notwithstanding), but I haven't wanted to deal with the breakup aftermath. My cell phone voice mail message is still the message that I and Melinda recorded together, the one that says we're "probably out hiking or taking Sawyer on a long walk," and far back in the fridge, there's a moldering container of strawberries, Melinda's favorite fruit, that I get nostalgic over every time I see it... So even though it's covered in mold and, at this point, contemplating growing eyes and walking out of my refrigerator, I've kept it there.

I'm stuck in a rut. And I know it.

That news story today was the last straw in an entire truckload of straws. My current job isn't my dream job, to put it mildly. I want to be a serious news anchor, not someone who reports on clown conventions.

Every inch of my apartment reminds me of my failed relationship (and Melinda made absolutely certain that I knew it was *my* fault that the relationship failed, before she stormed out two months ago).

My car is in the shop with a broken transmission that I can't afford to replace. I've been riding my bike to and from work and have a sunburn that I have to cover up with makeup whenever I'm on air...

Honestly, I try to remain optimistic. I've always been an optimistic person. But lately, it's been hard. Like, eating a carton of Ben & Jerry's every night and marathoning terrible Lifetime movies (and so much *Jeopardy!*) hard.

I wish it every hour on the hour, and I'm wishing it again now: I wish my mom was still around. I rinse Melinda's shampoo out of my hair and lean against the shower wall, pressing my forehead to its cool surface. Mom died two years ago, and ever since?

It feels like my life is out of balance.

⧗

As much as I'd like to, I can't wear a skirt on my bike. Well, I could, but there would probably be various and sundry humiliating ramifications that I just don't think I can deal with today — not on top of falling victim to a clown pie fight. So instead of the soft, cool blue dress that I was going to wear to Ginger's for dinner, I opt for some black jeans and a silky, slinky blue blouse that compliments my blue eyes.

Blue happens to be my favorite color — all shades of blue, really. Blue makes me think of the clear sky or open ocean, endless and full of possibilities, but I don't often get to wear blue at my job. For one, there's the blue screen problem, and for another, whenever I wear blue, Scott tells me that it makes my eyes look weird and alien on camera. So whenever I'm *not* at work, I seize every opportunity that I can to wear the color.

And, hey, blue fits my mood for today, too.

I clip my bike helmet onto my head and take my bike off the rack on the wall. "Be good," I tell Sawyer, who's already sprawled on the couch for the night, her face on her paws. She flops her tail once at me in a very halfhearted manner, and then I'm through the door, carrying my bike down the stairs.

Ginger's house is only ten minutes away, as the crow flies...or bikes. It's a nice, warm evening, but not too warm, and as I sit down on the bike and get my pedals going, the sun begins to slip down between the buildings, orange and purple arcing over the sky in a glorious display of color. It's going to be a spectacular sunset.

Despite the embarrassing broadcast that I'm never going to be able to live down—I can only imagine the treat I'm in for tomorrow morning when Dirk Dixon, who's even *more* of a jerk than his name would suggest, starts in on me with lewd whipped cream jokes that he's probably spending tonight dreaming up—I'm starting to feel more relaxed; bike riding always puts me in a better mood. It's just me and my bike, this glorious old cruiser that's more rust than metal, but it always gets me where I need to go. I glance down at the pavement, at my elongated shadow racing beside me on my bike, with a smile on my face...

Oh — wait.

What the heck?

There's another shadow. A shadow that most certainly isn't mine. It resembles the shadow of an enormous bird, but when I glance up, there's no bald eagle cruising above me. And there aren't any planes...

Seriously, what the *heck?*

I follow the shadow on the pavement right beside me with my eyes, but I can't find a single solid object nearby that might be casting it. And, besides, it looks like nothing I've ever seen before.

Honestly? I know this sounds crazy...

But it looks kind of like a person with wings.

Okay. One ticket to crazy town, coming right up. I take a deep breath, blink a couple of times, then glance down at the pavement again. The shadow is still there. And there's still no bald eagle above me.

And there's certainly no angel, either.

I think I've been way too stressed out lately. I wonder if whipped cream is toxic in high doses? Maybe I should start to take that yoga class that Ginger keeps asking me to try.

Maybe that'd help me destress...

But when I blink again, glance down again...the shadow is gone.

Yeah. I must have imagined it.

Obviously.

Definitely.

Still, there's a strange little feeling in my heart as I turn down the block toward Ginger's house. What *was* that? Could I have imagined something like that? Could I have *seriously* imagined an *angel* flying beside me on my bike? Why would such a weird idea have ever occurred to me?

But when I pull into Ginger's driveway, thoughts of strange, winged shadows vanish from my head.

Something's up.

Because there's a car parked beside Ginger's jeep in her driveway, a car that I've never seen before.

A sinking sensation starts to fill my chest, and I wheel the bike between the cars, pulling out the kickstand with my shoe and unclipping my bike helmet.

My suspicion may have been right: I have a feeling that Ginger *is* trying to set me up.

I mean, I'm not a hundred percent positive that this other car belongs to a lesbian who Ginger "just knows" would be "absolutely perfect" for me. But it's at least ninety nine percent probable. Ginger's done it before, after all, and she was just telling me last week that it's a shame that I'm still single, and she *did* ask me to wear something nice in her text...

And, let me be honest: Ginger does have my taste in ladies down pat.

But it doesn't matter if my dream woman is in Ginger's house right now, waiting for me to walk through that front door, to meet her and sweep her off her feet. I'm just not ready to date anyone yet. I know people say that and they don't actually mean it sometimes, but I really *do* mean it. I'm still dreaming about Melinda every night. Ginger knows this. But, then, Ginger loves to press an issue...

I ruffle my hair, trying to fluff it after the flattening the helmet caused as nervous butterflies begin to take wing in my stomach, fluttering against my rib cage in droves.

I know it sounds cliché, and a little naive, but it's true: I honestly thought Melinda was the *one* for me. We had plans, you know? Big plans. The kind of plans that end in church bells (well, metaphorically; I was never up for a church wedding) and white picket fences. Or, I guess, rainbow picket fences, in our case. We were going to adopt another dog together—Sawyer was always stubbornly *my* baby—spend every Christmas at a B&B in Vermont...

But then I caught Melinda in bed, *our* bed, with the wannabe actress barista Candace from my favorite coffee shop, Cuppa Jane. It's a female-run coffee shop, and a lot of the baristas are queer there—which kind of makes it the best place in the universe. Coffee. Lesbians. I mean, *really*. But I never (ever, *ever*) noticed any chemistry between Candace and Melinda when Melinda came in with me and ordered her standard vanilla latte. I was never looking for the little glances between them, because I believed that Melinda and I were going to be together forever.

I thought things were great between us, great chemistry, great sex...but then, I also thought I'd be a world-class television journalist traveling the planet to cover headlines by now. And, instead, I'm on the lowest rung of the smallest news station in the city.

I'm really beginning to doubt my own intuition.

I tug down the edges of my blue blouse, fluff my hair once more for good measure, though my normally wavy blonde hair remains obstinately limp on my shoulders. Then I wheel my bike into Ginger's garage and walk up to the front door.

I could always chicken out, bike straight back home, pedaling as quickly as the Wicked Witch in *The Wizard of Oz*...

I have that fleeting thought for a moment, but then I shake it out of my head.

With maximum reluctance, I press the doorbell. Normally I'd walk right on in; I have a key, after all. But I don't know what's waiting for me on the other side of that door, and I'd like to take a moment to orient myself.

I know that Ginger's scheming the moment that she answers the door, pulling it open in an elaborate *whoosh*.

Ginger Voorhees has long black hair that she normally draws up into a ponytail, beautiful brown eyes and gorgeous light brown skin. Honestly, everything about Ginger is gorgeous, from her smile and the way she laughs to the adorable way her nose wrinkles when one of the kids on her Little League team does something (as she calls it) "silly."

The only reason I first spoke to Ginger during our freshman year of college was because I was working up the courage to ask her out. But Ginger is tragically straight, and that is probably a good thing. We've been inseparable friends for more than a decade, and if she been datable, I probably would have burned that bridge a long time ago.

Ginger stands in the doorway now, narrowing the opening and wedging her curvy body tightly into the small space, so that I can't see beyond her. "Hi!" she tells me cheerfully. "Um...how are you?" she asks, wincing a little — probably because her question sounds absurdly cheerful.

I lift a single brow, cross my arms over my chest, and tilt my head to the side.

"Uh, come in, come in," she tells me in an extra-loud voice, enunciating, most likely, for the benefit of whoever else is in the house, waiting for me. "Why don't you come into the *dining room*, actually?" Ginger says, projecting her voice loudly enough to audition for a stage production. She reaches out, grasping my wrist and tugging me into her house.

We trot down the hallway, and then, in a matter of seconds, I'm ushered into the dining room...

And there's a pretty woman with short black hair I've never seen before, standing by the large mahogany table.

"Erin," says Ginger, her tone syrupy. I glance at her, my brow still raised. "This is Rachel Gomez. Rachel? This is Erin McEvoy. Why don't you two have a seat while I finish making dinner?" Ginger encourages the both of us with a wide smile, and then she scampers through the door that leads to the kitchen, shutting it firmly behind her.

The woman, Rachel, flashes me a brilliant smile and shrugs delicately. "That's Ginger for you. It's nice to meet you, Erin," she tells me, holding out her hand.

I shake it with an uncertain smile. "It's nice to meet you, too, Rachel. I'm sorry. I'm just surprised that there's another guest for dinner. I thought it was just going to be Ginger and me tonight."

"I'm sorry, too," says Rachel, her smile warming. "I had no idea Ginger was trying to set me up... But I'm pretty sure she is," she laughs lightly.

I relax a little, laughing, too, as I feel my shoulders release their tension. "Yeah, Ginger's a born matchmaker."

Rachel smiles and shakes her head. "Wine?" she asks me, gesturing to the bottles of red and white wine situated in the center of the dining room table.

In addition to coaching Little League, Ginger is utterly obsessed with Major League Baseball. The Red Sox, to be precise. Their logo is emblazoned on the red tablecloth, and the two wine glasses on the table are etched with the Red Sox logo.

"Yeah, I'd love some red," I tell Rachel with a smile, sitting down across from her at the table. "It'd have to be red, right?" I quip, gesturing around to all of the Red Sox memorabilia decorating the room.

Rachel chuckles. She's very pretty when she laughs. And I can admire her in the way you might admire a beautiful painting. But there's absolutely nothing going on in my head or in my heart when I gaze at Rachel Gomez.

Worried, I wonder how long it's going to take me to get over Melinda...

"Please don't be offended, but I really want to get this out of the way," says Rachel then, her eyes warm as she watches me. Her words are surprising, but her tone is soft, soothing. I smile at her with wide eyes. "I just broke up with my girlfriend a week ago," she tells me with a small grimace, "and I don't think I'm ready to date anyone new yet."

"Oh, of course," I tell her, relaxing completely now; she hands me the full wine glass. "I totally understand," I tell her with a smile. "I broke up with my girlfriend recently, too, and it's hard for me. The pain's still fresh. I'm not ready for a new relationship, either."

"Well, we make a fine pair, don't we?" says Rachel with a chuckle, leaning back in the dining room chair. "Ginger and I work together at the Museum of Fine Arts," she tells me, taking a sip of wine and rolling the ruby liquid around in the glass. "You look familiar, actually..." she muses me, her head to the side. "How do you know Ginger?"

"College," I tell her with a small smirk. "Would you believe that I asked her out? She turned me down nicely, then asked me to go have drinks in a friendship-type way because—quote—she admired my guts. The rest is history..."

"And where do you work?" asks Rachel, smiling.

Sheepishly, I shake my head and laugh, but it's a strained laugh. This is the question I dread answering. I cough, then force out, "Do you ever watch BEAN?" I spell the acronym reluctantly.

Rachel sits forward, her eyes alight. "That's *it!* I saw the story you did in Peabody a few weeks back. It was sweet, how you helped those kids get their cat out of the tree."

I wince a little, swirling the wine in my glass. Then I shake my head, chagrined. "Yeah, what you *didn't* see on air was that I spent the night in the hospital with cat scratch fever — which, oddly enough, isn't covered by workers' comp," I tell her with a chuckle.

The bee stings and subsequent urgent care visit resulting from the apiary story I reported on two months ago weren't covered by workers' comp, either. And, now that I think of it, neither were the doctor's bills from the case of measles I developed after covering a story about a preschool's Christmas pageant. At this point, my job is probably costing me more money than it earns me. And it's becoming a threat to my health.

The strains of a classical song chirp out cheerfully from Rachel's jeans pocket. She gets up, brows furrowed, as she takes her phone out, staring at the screen in shock. "Excuse me, please," she tells me with another warm smile; then she moves out into the hallway to take the call.

I lift my wine glass to my lips. I'm trying not to eavesdrop, but the hallway is only three feet away, so I can hear Rachel loud and clear.

"Baby, I'm sorry, too," she says, her voice chocked with emotion. "I miss you so much..."

The soft way that Rachel's speaking, the warmth, the pain evident in her voice... She could only be talking to her ex. I bite my lip, stare down at the Red Sox logo on the tablecloth.

"Yeah, I'm kind of at a thing right now, but if you really want me to come, maybe I can—yes. I'll be right there. I..." Rachel says this all in a rush, then draws in a deep breath. "I still love you," she murmurs tenderly.

She says a few other things, quieter things, and then I hear Rachel say, "I'll see you very soon," before she hangs up. I'm blushing bright crimson when she walks back into the dining room—not because I was listening in on her conversation but because red wine always makes me blush...*and* because the way that Rachel was talking to her ex? It was so soft. So warm. So gentle. So affectionate.

And so full of love.

God, I miss that. I want that. And that want, that need, lances through my body, hitting me hard in the heart.

"I'm so sorry," Rachel says with a shake of her head, cradling her phone in her hands like it's something precious. There are tears standing in her eyes as she shakes her head again. "I'm so sorry, Erin. It was so nice to meet you... Can you please give my apologies to Ginger? I've got to go right now. That was—"

"I know. It's totally fine. I'll tell Ginger," I say, giving Rachel a big smile. "You go get your girl." I throw her a salute.

Rachel appreciates the gesture, nods and, with an eager smile, turns on her heels and practically skips into the hallway. Then she's through the front door.

"Well, how are you two getting along..." begins Ginger, sweeping through the kitchen door with a steaming, mouth-watering bowl of alfredo penne pasta. She halts in the doorway, arm around the hot dish, her head tilted to the side. "Where's Rachel?" she mouths to me.

"Rachel had to go," I tell her, setting my empty wine glass down in front of me. "She's getting back together with her ex-girlfriend. God, that smells good. I'm starved..."

I reach for the bowl in her hands, but Ginger is only staring at me, blinking. Okay, she probably needs a little more explanation.

"Rachel got a phone call," I tell Ginger with a smile and a shrug. "From her ex. They apparently have a lot of unresolved business and still love each other, so Rachel just left—to go sweep her ex off her feet."

"Well, that's...unexpected," she says, furrowing her brow. "But, I mean, good for her. Rachel was really hung up on that woman, so, yeah, all's well that ends well, I guess." She gives me a small frown. "Sorry about that. I really did think she was perfect for you."

I wave the apology off with a smile; but then I put my chin in my hands and sigh. "Ginger?"

"Yeah, honey?" asks Ginger, placing the bowl of pasta right in front of me.

I inhale deeply, then sigh again. "Do you think I'll ever have anything like that?" Ginger gives me a sort of perplexed look, so I turn my hand slowly in the air. "You know, like what Rachel and her ex have?"

"It can't have been that wonderful, sweetie. They *did* break up," says Ginger, brow raised, but then she goes back into the kitchen to grab a plate of garlic bread, calling out over her shoulder, "But if that's what you want—"

"Okay, obviously, the grass is always greener," I tell her, as she sets the plate of garlic bread down next to the pasta. I take a huge whiff of that, too, and sag back against the chair. "God, Ginger, that smells *so* good—"

"Thanks. You were saying?" she asks wryly, sitting down across from me and pouring some red wine into her own glass.

"So, the grass is always greener," I repeat, as Ginger refills my wine glass to the brim. "And their relationship looks perfect to me because I'm not *in* a relationship, and I'm not in *that* relationship, so I don't know what's really going on with them…"

I'm babbling. I know I'm babbling, but

I'm trying to find the thread of something important, something that I need to express to my best friend.

"But I want *something*," I tell her finally. "Something that makes me have the same look on my face that Rachel had when she picked up the phone. Something that makes my voice go all soft, like hers did when she was talking to her ex. Something full of warmth and connection. You know?"

"Not really," says Ginger, her chin in her hands, an amused smile on her face.

"I want to be loved," I tell her breathlessly, "and I want to love someone so much that...that..." I brandish the wine glass, spreading my arms, "that I'd drop anything, anytime, anywhere, to be near them. That I couldn't imagine my life without them. That...that..." I take a deep breath, my eyes misting up. "I want to be so in love that I feel complete," I finally whisper.

Ginger lifts her glass. "I can drink to that," she tells me gently, and we *clink* our wine glasses together. We take long sips of our wine, and I can feel my face flush more deeply, the wine coursing through my body.

"Anyway," Ginger tells me, spooning pasta onto my plate, "I'm sorry about setting you up on a blind date like that." She winces a little and offers me an apologetic smile. "You've just been so down lately, and I thought a new romantic interest might pull you up out of the dumps. I mean...Rachel *was* super hot, right?" she asks me teasingly.

"Right," I tell her with a little grin, shoveling a forkful of too-hot pasta into my mouth. "And you know I appreciate the thought, Ging." And I do—I appreciate, so much, that Ginger is always looking out for me. I take a deep breath, my fork dangling in mid-air before I set it back down on the plate. "But Melinda bruised me pretty badly, and I'm still just... I'm still a little too hurt to start dating again."

"Hey, then what was that whole sweeping speech about? The one you delivered, like, a minute ago? About wanting to be loved?" asks Ginger, handing over the plate of garlic bread.

The warmth of the wine is still flowing through me, but the spark that I felt a moment ago is gone, vanished. I shake my head. "I do want that. I want it..." I tell her quietly. "But I don't think I'm ready for it. Not yet."

Ginger sighs in exasperation. "Erin." She says my name warningly, and I glance at her with a half-smile. "Don't talk yourself out of good things, okay, babe?" she tells me, reaching across the table to take my hand and squeeze it. "I'm *serious*," she says, when I roll my eyes a little. "You have this terrible habit of thinking too much about everything, analyzing everything, and then the good things just never happen—because you've analyzed the *hell* out of the situation and the situation's already passed you by. You know what I'm saying?"

"Not really," I quip, taking another sip of wine.

But I do know what she's saying.

I think too much before I act; I make pros-and-cons lists about the most inconsequential decisions, and when there's a woman involved, I overexamine *everything*. I've been trying to get better about that tendency, but I am who I am...

And sometimes, I'm afraid that this bad habit means that I'm going to be lonely for the rest of my life. That, whenever there's an opportunity for a relationship with an amazing woman, I'm going to let it pass me by because I've spent too much time wondering if she's "the one."

Ginger changes the topic of conversation to lighten the mood, and soon we're chatting about mutual friends and Ginger's current love interest—which is a much more interesting subject than my current singlehood. Ginger has been dating Oliver, a really nice guy who works at the museum with her, for a couple of months now, and they're planning a romantic getaway to Hawaii together. A major trip... That's usually a sign that Ginger is getting serious about someone. And I'm so happy for her. Ginger deserves to be in a relationship with someone who treats her like the world wonder she is. And Oliver does exactly that.

"Are you sure you're all right to bike?" Ginger asks me, concerned, after dinner—and three more glasses of wine. But I've been drinking over the course of several hours; I think I'm fine. I'm surprised to see that it's nearly midnight when I glance up at the clock.

"Don't worry, Ging," I tell her with a big smile. Biking and driving a car are two very different activities, after all, and I'm pretty sure I can get back to my apartment in one piece if I take the ride nice and slow, despite my tipsy state.

Ginger kisses me on the cheek and shoos me out the door with a Tupperware full of her delicious, homemade alfredo pasta, which I'm probably going to eat for breakfast. "Be careful!" she admonishes me, before calling out, "Good night!"

I stumble into her garage and pat the seat of my bike muzzily. It takes me two tries to swing my leg up and over the seat, and another two tries to set the Tupperware container full of pasta into my front basket, but finally I peel out the driveway into the soothing, cool dark of a suburban Boston night.

I'm pedaling along, enjoying the night breeze. At the first major intersection, I fail to notice that my light already turned red. Whoops. I sail through the intersection, unable to stop; luckily, there weren't any cars coming from the cross road. Still, a little thrill of fear races through me as I realize how awful that mistake could have been if a car, or something bigger, had been barreling toward me.

I take a deep breath and keep peddling, blinking back the wind-tears and trying to pay closer attention to my surroundings. At the next intersection, I slow down as the light turns yellow; then I cruise to a stop.

There are a lot of bicyclists who ignore traffic lights and street signs, but, *technically*, you're supposed to obey them, just as a car would. Still, once I see that there aren't vehicles approaching from any direction, I ease out into the intersection, peddling my bike forward.

And that's when I hear the car horn.

What the heck? That car came from out of *nowhere*. For some reason, it doesn't have its lights on. I pump my right peddle, trying to gain momentum and speed after standing still; adrenaline rushes through me, but I'm too tired, and I don't have enough thrust. The car lights flick on, glaring my vision, while the car horn still blares in my ears, and I realize, in that instant, that there's nothing I can do to escape this: the car is going to hit me.

But then...something really weird happens.

I'm pushed from behind. It's the same sensation I used to get when I was a kid and my mom pushed me on the playground swing. That's the only way I can make sense of it in my head... I'm trying to pedal my bike forward, and I get *shoved* in the small of my back, and then the bike is careening forward quickly. So quickly, in fact, that I avoid the car narrowly, so narrowly that the bike wobbles beneath me in the wake of the speeding car's air.

I blink, turn around in my seat.

There are streetlights everywhere; the road itself is pretty well lit. I *know* I was pushed, pushed just enough that I escaped from the car unharmed. I felt warm hands on the small of my back before I was shoved forward.

But there's no one here. No one behind me. No one at all on the deserted street.

I slow down, stop, pausing for a long moment, trying to figure out what just happened to me. But I can't figure it out. There's no logical explanation. So, finally, perplexed, I start pedaling again down the road, adrenaline spiking through me after such a close call.

I try to take in deep breaths of air, try to calm my racing heartbeat. I think, for a moment, that I glimpse that weird winged shadow from before gliding on the pavement beside me. It seems as if there's a darker spot there, a moving black mass that I catch in the corner of my eye. But I when I look down at the street, then look up into the sky...there's nothing there. No bird. No shadow. There's nothing there at all.

I'm pretty creeped out but, all in all, glad to be alive. When I finally reach my apartment, I lug my bike up the stairs, open the door and sit down on the couch next to Sawyer.

"It's been a crazy day, sweetheart," I tell my dog, who thumps her tail against the couch cushion politely for a moment before falling back to sleep.

I take another shower to clear my head from the excess wine. It doesn't help, but I'm so relieved to be home, to be safe that, when I fall into bed, I just lie there for a long moment, staring up at the ceiling before fishing out my much-abused, torn paperback from beneath my pillow.

The Princess and Her Lady Knight is one of my favorite romances of all time, and though I know the book by heart, I need something familiar and comforting right now. Since, you know, I almost got hit by a car.

But as I begin to read the first page, I get the oddest feeling—like I'm being watched. I glance around the room, but Sawyer, the only creature who *could* be watching me, hasn't left her spot on the couch.

It's just me in the bedroom. Just me.

I rub my eyes tiredly and put my book back under the pillow, shutting off the light.

I really need to sleep.

Still, it takes me an hour or so to drift off. Behind my closed lids, I keep seeing that winged shadow on the ground. And I keep feeling those impossible hands on my back, pushing me out of harm's way.

⌛

Unsurprisingly, I dream about angels.
Well, *one* angel.
I'm sitting on a puffy cloud, because that's dream logic for you. I'm wearing a long white dress with pleats, '80s-style, with a slim gold belt looped around my waist, white flats on my feet. The sunshine, cartoonish rays beaming down, is extra-bright, infusing the world with a friendly yellow glow.

Everything is so bright, in fact, that I have to lift my hand to shield my eyes.

And that's when I realize that I'm not alone. There's someone sitting next to me on the cloud.

She has wings. Huge, fluffy, white wings, the exact kind of wings you'd expect an angel to have. I notice her wings first, because her back is to me.

But then she turns, and I draw in a deep breath.

She has dark, shoulder-length hair that brushes against the edges of her shoulders in satiny waves. Her bright, beautiful smile dazzles me as much as the sunshine. She's wearing a white suit with a white tie, and my dream self recognizes that as super hot, especially with those glorious wings.

But the thing that I really notice, that draws me in like a beacon...

Her eyes.

Weirdly enough, they're bright turquoise.

Who has turquoise eyes? I feel like I've seen them before.

"Hello, Erin," the angel tells me, her voice low, a growl that makes me shiver.

The scene ends abruptly: the angel parts her lips, as if she's about to tell me something. Suddenly, I'm no longer on a white, fluffy cloud; I'm walking Sawyer on the sidewalk. There's a guy wearing a dancing hot dog costume in front of my favorite diner...and the dream just gets stranger from there.

But when I wake in the morning, sitting up in bed and raking a hand through my tangled hair, the only image I remember clearly is the angel.

The angel and her turquoise eyes.

Chapter 2: The Angel Wears Sneakers

It's been a rough week.

On top of all of the ribbing I got from my co-workers about the pie-in-the-face incident, I've been forced to cover 1) a baked bean-eating contest—which resulted in someone throwing up on my shoes; which resulted in me having to throw said shoes out. 2) A book fair, whose spokesperson was afflicted with a terrible case of stage fright and stricken mute on camera. When the poor woman fainted, we had to call an EMT. 3) And a turtle race—which was actually kind of adorable, albeit very wet. Rain and thunder during the whole live broadcast.

And, most unsettling of all, I keep seeing that shadow. That *winged* shadow.

I see it everywhere: on the sidewalks, roads, even in the hallways here at the station. The shadow has been my near-constant companion, drifting along the carpeting or the pavement, on fence posts and the sides of buildings, always hovering just behind me or beside me, depending on the direction of the light...

But that's absurd. Because there is no being *attached* to the shadow. Nothing that a source of light should be able to create a shadow *from*. There's just...nothing. There's never any solid or moving object nearby when the shadow appears.

I have an appointment with an optometrist next week to have my eyes checked thoroughly. I've always had 20/20 vision, but what else could be causing this to happen? What else could be causing that shadow — other than a strange anomaly with my eyes?

Well, I could be delusional, I guess, but that's something I'm not prepared to consider right now. Though I may have to consider it. Because something else happened yesterday, something that's making me question my sanity.

I was standing in the work bathroom, and I grabbed a paper towel to wipe my wet hands. When I glanced up into the mirror, I thought I saw... I thought I glimpsed someone else's reflection in the mirror, right beside mine. But I turned around, and there was no one behind me, because no one else was in the bathroom. And when I looked again at the mirror, I saw only my own reflection staring back at me — wide-eyed, a little frightened.

The really weird thing is that the reflection of the person I thought I saw...she looked just like the angel that I dreamed about. And I only dreamed about the angel once, but I can't seem to stop thinking about her. She keeps popping up in my thoughts...

Is that crazy? I mean, more crazy than seeing the reflection of a dream woman in the mirror? More crazy than seeing a shadow that's not there? I worry that I'm becoming paranoid. I always feel as if I'm being watched. It started that night, the night of the almost-accident. I had a feeling that I was being watched in my bedroom, and that hair-rising-on-the-back-of-my-neck feeling hasn't gone away since.

I sit at my desk at the station now, tapping an unsharpened pencil against my desktop keyboard, dreading my next assignment and worrying about my mental health. Really, though, that's just another day at BEAN.

Scott's sitting across from me at his desk, and we keep exchanging glances with one another. Occasionally, he'll raise an eyebrow and make a funny face, and I'll grin at him in return. I look at the clock on my monitor: almost noon.

It's usually around noon that we get our reporting assignments.

"What do you think it'll be today?" asks Scott. He's leaning back in his chair, his hands behind his head as he stretches. "Do you want to put money on the possibility that it'll involve a cute animal?"

"Hey, the cute animal stories are almost all right," I tell him with a small smile. "It's the weird-slash-creepy stories that are beginning to rub me the wrong way."

"Yeah, it's like the whole station thinks we have no talent for reporting on real news," says Scott, with a sigh and a shrug. "But whatever," he offers, with his usual optimism. "We keep on truckin', right, partner?"

"Sure," I smile.

Like me, Scott has higher aspirations than working at BEAN, the smallest news station in Boston. He has dreams of moving to Hollywood someday and becoming a movie cameraman, which I have no doubt in the world that he could do. But, right now, he and Sylvia and sweet little Lulu are biding their time in Boston until Sylvia finishes up her medical internship.

"I shall go forth and get chips, milady," says Scott, standing and stretching again. "Do you want chips of potato or chips of corn?" He's affecting a pretty strong Ren Faire accent.

I don't know what I'm going to do with myself when Scott leaves BEAN. I'll be happy for him, of course, but how will I be able to bear another clown convention without my faithful camera guy—who, whenever he heads to the vending machine, always buys chips for two?

But my growling stomach can't wait any longer. "No chips for me, but thank you, Scott. You're as chivalrous as ever," I tell him, grabbing my purse from under my desk and standing up. "I think I'm going to hit up the deli. If we get a call out, just text me and pick me up there."

He nods, heading out the door for the vending machine.

"Hey, do you want anything from the deli?" I call after him.

Scott turns, and his eyes glaze over with expectant happiness as he fixes me with an enormous smile. He was totally waiting for me to ask. "Could you get me one of those huge pickles?" he asks, almost reverently.

I laugh. I've never met anyone in the world who loves pickles as much as Scott, but I have to agree—the pickles at All That and a Bag of Chips are really, well, all that. First off, they're *enormous*, and they have a spectacular crunch.

"I promise I'll bring one back for you," I tell him, and then I move around my desk and out of the oppressive office, down the corridor and into the bright, happy sunshine of a summer day. It isn't *too* hot, and there are puffy white clouds in the sky. The birds are singing, and everyone on the streets seems to be wearing a smile. Or...maybe that's just my perception now that I've escaped from BEAN's dark, dingy building.

I put my earbuds in my ears and turn on the audiobook app on my phone. The deli is only a couple of blocks away, but I'm going to savor my lunch break, and part of that savoring involves listening to my current obsession, a steamy romance novel called *Her Heart's Queen*. It's about a queen who falls in love with a gorgeous fairy warrior woman from a rival land.

"My queen," the warrior woman said, kneeling at her feet. "You are my beloved. All my heart and all that I am belongs to you—" The woman's eyes took on a glint of lust as her fingers traced a line up the queen's bare thigh...

I'm a little flustered as I stand at the intersection, thinking about that fairy warrior woman and her exploring fingers. I'm so distracted, in fact, that when the *walk* sign lights up, I don't look both ways. You know, that little habit that was drilled into your brain when you were a child—to *always* look both ways before you cross a street, no matter what.

I don't do it.

I'm too distracted. I'm stepping out into the intersection mechanically, concentrating on the audiobook, concentrating on the hot-and-steamy moment between the two main characters.

And...it's strange. For a moment, the narration fades away, and I can't hear a thing. Everything just falls silent. That being-watched feeling intensifies, the pricking on the back of my neck growing more palpable. I turn a little, surprised, and that's when I see something that fills me with a sickening dose of *deja vu*.

A car is barreling toward me from the

right, running the red light. It's coming too fast to stop, too fast to swerve. There is no way that I'm going to be able to avoid it. It's like I'm stuck in taffy or glue; I can't can't lift a finger, can't even blink. Everything is happening too fast, and the car is almost on top of me.

The other people at the intersection, I realize now, lagged back because they saw this car aiming to run the red light. They're shouting at me, have probably been shouting at me for a while, but the audiobook was too loud in my ears, and I hadn't been paying attention, and now it's too late. The car is almost here, poised to slam into my thighs, and—in that still, endless moment—my entire life really does flash in front of my eyes.

I know that people say that happens in near-death accidents, but I always thought it was a figure of speech, a tired cliché. And what does it really *mean*, anyway, to have your life flash in front of your eyes?

I find out, because that's exactly what happens to me.

I don't see my *entire* life, not really. Just choice bits and pieces, my favorite moments, and some of my not-so favorite ones, too. There's the time that I asked Ginger out for the drink, and there's the time that Melinda and I first had sex, totally drunk and laughing inappropriately as we kissed one another, as I fell on top of her, stone drunk and in the dark.

There's the moment that I got hired at BEAN; I had a huge smile on my face, excited and hopeful that everything was going to turn out great, that this job was the first stepping stone on the road to to my dream...

And then here I am, standing in the center of the intersection, about to be run over by a car. I'm present in the here and now again as I wince, bracing for impact.

And something *does* hit me. Hard.

But...wouldn't a car hit harder?

No... Wait. No, I wasn't hit by a car. I was shoved off of the road again, something smacking so forcefully against me that I'm lifted from my feet, propelled across the pavement through the air, and I'm on the other side of the street suddenly, lying on the sidewalk.

Impossibly, I landed as lightly as if I were a feather in the wind.

Because whatever ran into me *carried* me here—and then set me down gently.

I open my eyes, eyes that I clenched tight against the collision, against the sight of my own imminent death. I stare at the sky, adrenaline pouring through me as I pant, trying to breathe, trying to take in that I'm alive, that I survived—a fact that's proving hard to believe.

And that's when I realize that there's a face about an inch away from my own.

Adrenaline surges through me again. I'm hardly breathing, and suddenly I feel like I'm floating, weightless...

Because the face above me is beautiful, more than beautiful.

She's...*shining*. As if a faint golden mist is edging the outline of this woman, this woman crouching over me, this woman who, I can only assume, just saved me from being flattened in the intersection.

This woman who looks *exactly* like the angel in my dream.

"It's not possible," I whisper, and before I can tell myself not to, I'm reaching up, brushing my fingertips across her right cheek, utterly convinced that my hand is about to move through air, that I've imagined her, just like I imagined her reflection in the bathroom mirror at BEAN. My fingers should brush against the nothingness of a fantasy.

But my fingertips press against solid, soft, warm flesh.

She's real. *Real.*

The slight shimmer to the air around her, that pale golden mist, intensifies for a moment, as if I'm staring at the sun. I blink, move my hand to my eyes, and when I open my eyes again, that shimmer and mist are gone.

But the woman remains.

Her incredible turquoise eyes—eyes that dive deep inside of me, that must make my own blue eyes look gray by comparison—sweep up and down the length of my body...slowly, bright gaze burning. A hot blush warms my cheeks. Her gaze finally settles on my own eyes again, and she bends her face a little closer to mine.

She gives me a small smile, then, her playful-looking mouth (something about the way her mouth curves so makes her look as if she smiles a *lot*) turning up at the corners, as she asks in a low, husky voice, "All right, Erin?"

I nod before I realize that I'm conversing with a figment of my imagination, or someone who, at least, *was* a figment of my imagination until recently.

The woman rises to her feet smoothly, straightening the front of her black pinstripe suit jacket. Oddly, she's wearing white sneakers with the formal-style suit. I've never *seen* sneakers so white.

She bends down now, offers me a warm hand, which I take before my mind catches up with my body. But she's already helping me stand up.

Her hand is so warm in mine, so strong and feather-soft. There's something about this woman's air that makes me think of feathers...

Suddenly the sights and sounds and smells of summer in Boston all come rushing straight at me—including the sight of a car with a busted fender smoking in the middle of the intersection, exactly where I'd been standing before the car had been about to hit me.

Oh. The car with the busted fender *is* the

car that had been about to hit me.

But...it *didn't* hit me. So why is its fender bent inward, as if it hit...something?

The driver of the car is on the road, staring down at the damage, swearing visibly while he crosses and uncrosses his arms. When he catches my eye, he nods toward me.

"Hey, you all right, lady?" he asks with a jerk of his chin.

"I...think so," I answer vaguely. I glance down at my legs, make sure they're still attached. So far, so good.

The woman beside me casts me an amused glance, her mouth curving upward—and the sight of that smile is like sunshine streaming from behind a storm cloud.

Really, it's exactly like that.

"Well, that's a good day's work, then," she says, in her low, husky voice.

A voice that, I have to admit, makes me feel a little weak in the knees.

I blink. Then: "What?" I ask her, confused.

I'm even more confused by what she does next.

She tilts her head back, bright turquoise eyes pointed toward the sky, frowning. She says nothing, only stares up, gaze narrowed, head tilted to one side, like she's...*listening* for something.

After a long, motionless moment of

staring at this woman staring at the sky, she tilts her chin down at last, blinks and sighs heavily. She shoves her hands into her pockets, casting one more glance up, eyes narrowed again. "Really?" she says.

But she's not talking to me.

She's talking to...the sky. To the clouds. To...up there.

"*Really?*" she mutters again, this time sarcastically, and she groans and runs a long-fingered hand through her hair before she shakes her head in frustration. "You're *sure* that wasn't the big one?" she says again, still talking to the sky. "*Really* sure? Because that was *awfully* close, and if I hadn't—"

"Um." I clear my throat a little desperately. The woman casts her gaze down to meet mine, one brow raised. "Who are you talking to?" I ask her, with a weak smile.

The woman regards me with a small, mysterious curve to her lips. "Right. Now, tell me something," she says, sliding both hands into her suit jacket pockets and angling her shoulders toward me. "Are you especially, uh, accident prone?" she asks, her head angled to the side, her smile widening as if she's gazing at a particularly interesting problem that she wants to solve.

"What?" I shake my head.

"Never mind," she says with a shrug and a sigh. "I *thought* I just saved your life, but it turns out I *didn't*, so—"

I hold up my hands. "Stop. Slow down." She does stop, staring at me with wide eyes, as if she's surprised that I interrupted her. I ask the very first question that comes to mind: "How did you know my name?" And then: "Who *are* you?"

"Ah." The woman nods her head, still smiling brightly. "Sorry, sorry. I'm kind of new at this. Well—not *new*. More like new*ish*. I mean, I've been at it for three centuries, but in Seraphic time, that's, oh, about the length of a nice hot bath here on Earth."

I blink. Feel faint. Blink again. Wobble a little on my feet.

Did she say, *Seraphic*? As *in...seraphim?* Angels?

"I...can't understand a word you're saying," I tell her, the adrenaline pooling down into my feet and leaving me exhausted. I take a deep breath. "But thank you," I say, meaning it.

"For what?" asks the woman, her mouth set in a bemused half-frown, half-smile.

I gesture back toward the road, where traffic is moving normally again, the guy in the damaged car having already driven away, bent fender notwithstanding. I guess once he saw that I was okay, he didn't want to stick around in case I became sue-happy. I take another deep breath.

"Correct me if I'm wrong, but..." I stare at

this woman, this impossible woman. She's a bit taller than me, so I have to lift my chin to meet her eyes, which I do, all the while thinking, *Those must be contact lenses...* "I nearly got hit by a car a moment ago. I...think." I turn my hand around in mid-air, trying to find the words, spluttering. "I mean, it happened so fast, I'm not even sure. And then you just *appeared* —"

"Well, I didn't just *appear*. I was already there, technically."

"What do you—"

"And the fact of the matter is, apparently"—she casts her eyes heavenward with a doubtful smile—"you would've survived whether I'd crashed into you or not." She nods in a very business-like manner, as if we're in the midst of a corporate meeting. "So no thanks necessary, Erin."

I lick my lips, speechless.

"Bu-u-u-ut," she continues, drawing out the word as the sexiest, sliest grin moves over her face, "since I've gone physical and revealed myself to you, I'm afraid we're going to be stuck together for the next..." She pauses to check a watch-like device on her wrist. It *looks* like a watch, but it's a lot clunkier than any watch I've ever seen. Maybe it's one of those new smart watches? "Well, for the next three to four weeks, I'd guess. Sorry I can't be more specific than that, but fate isn't an exact science—or so *they* tell me."

"*They?*" Out of everything she just said, speaking so quickly that I got a headache trying to keep up with her, my brain latched onto that one small word. "They *who?*"

"Just...*them*. You know." She points up toward the sky, both of her brows raised. "Anyway, you were on your way to lunch. It's this way, isn't it?" She nods to the right and offers her arm, as if she's a gentleman in an old-time movie. Dazed and confused, I accept her arm, threading my hand through the crook of her elbow.

She knew I was on my way to lunch, which direction I was aiming for... And, as we walk down the street together and the woman ducks through the front door of All That and a Bag of Chips, pulling me behind her, I realize that, somehow, she knew exactly where I intended to go for lunch.

Impossible.

And where did that dent in the fender come from? It was a large dent, a person-shaped dent. Did the car actually *hit* this woman when she pushed me out of the way? If so, why isn't she dead? *How could she have saved me?* The car was moving far too fast... Only Superman is capable of such a feat—and Superman isn't real.

Around and around my thoughts spin as we both sit down in my favorite booth of the deli. I exhale heavily, letting my purse drop off of my shoulder onto the seat beside me. Then I stare across the table at the woman who—despite her protestations—just saved my life.

The woman from my dream.

"Hey, lady!" says Cheryl, my favorite waitress here. I've been coming to All That and a Bag of Chips for so long that Cheryl and I have become good friends. When she glances at me now, her brows angle upward as she looks from me to the dark-haired woman in my booth. She taps her pen against her pad of paper. "Uh...do you want the usual? Do you want me to come back? Are you all right?" The last question is spoken in a low whisper, Cheryl leaning down so that her golden curls brush against my cheek. "You look a little green."

I glance sidelong at Cheryl. Her kind, brown eyes meet my own widened gaze, and then I mumble, "I'll just have the usual, thanks."

"One grilled cheese-and-tomato-flavored pile of homemade potato chips coming right up." Cheryl glances at my companion. "And for you?"

"I'll have the same," the woman replies bemusedly.

"All righty," says Cheryl, taking a step backwards. She shoots me an, *Is everything really okay?* expression, and I nod at her before she turns around to head toward the kitchen.

"So." I lick my dry lips, feeling like a bundle of nerves. In contrast, the woman has her arms crossed, leaning back in the booth as if she's perfectly comfortable going out to lunch with a stranger she just saved from death. "Are you going to tell me who you are..." I trail off, watching her. "Or—"

"Of course!" She nods smoothly, leaning forward. "Where are my manners?" Then she holds out her hand, says, "My name is Gabrielle, a Seraphim of the Ninth Order—Ninth being the lowest order, but, just between you and me, I'm hoping to work my way up to Eighth with this assignment."

I stare at her for a long moment. "Seraphim," I finally whisper, laughing weakly.

"Perhaps you've never heard of—"

"No, I've heard of seraphim. They're, like, angels, but—"

"Not *like* angels," Gabrielle grins, leaning back in the booth again. Okay, she's probably going to tell me that *Seraphim* is the name of a local sports team, or orchestra, or acting troupe, or band. I start to relax, but she's shaking her head.

"I'm an *angel*," she says simply. "You can't be *like* something you are. Human language is a bit tricky, isn't it?" She chuckles thoughtfully.

I stare at her with wider eyes.

This woman, this woman seated across from me, actually believes that she's an angel. And I have no idea how to respond to that.

I'm not religious. But even if I *were*

63

religious, I find it hard to believe that there are people with wings, dressed all in white, sitting on clouds and looking out for the Earthlings far below.

Gabrielle isn't even dressed in white. She's wearing a black-and-white pinstripe suit. Granted, her shirt and shoes are white, but...

Stop, Erin. Am I really trying to justify this woman's claim? True, I *did* dream about someone who looked like her, and the woman in my dream happened to have angel wings, but—

"So," says Gabrielle, her head tilted to one side. "What did we just order for lunch? I'm a big fan of lunch—second only to brunch."

The change of subject startles me, and I answer her question in a robotic-sounding voice: "You ordered a plate of homemade potato chips. They're flavored like grilled cheese and tomato."

Gabrielle looks a little stunned. "A *plate* of homemade potato chips?"

"It's a potato chip restaurant," I tell her, smiling a little as I gesture to the diner around us. "They only serve potato chips and pickles here."

Gabrielle's mouth falls open, but then she shuts it again, her face lighting up with such a big smile that she seems to practically glow. "Well, *what* will they think of next? Maybe the world really is worth saving, after all," she tells me with a soft smile, crossing her arms in front of her.

"Um...thanks?" I manage, as Cheryl comes trotting out from the back with two enormous plates of potato chips, the customary small jar of pickles balanced expertly on her forearm as she navigates the plates toward us.

"Enjoy," she tells us with a flourish, clinking the plates down and opening the jar of pickles before placing it between us. Then she darts away to answer the inquiries of a man and woman who just wandered into the restaurant and who—like Gabrielle—are finding it a little hard to believe that a restaurant could exist that serves only homemade, gourmet potato chips.

"What are these?" asks Gabrielle, leaning forward with wide, shining eyes to lift the jar of pickles.

I pause, my hand holding a potato chip halfway to my mouth as I stare at her. "They're...pickles," I say, setting the potato chip down. "You don't know what pickles are?"

Gabrielle stares down into the jar before fishing one out expertly and holding it in front of her. It sags limply to the side, and the scent of vinegar makes my mouth begin to water.

"You eat these, I presume?" she asks, flicking an eager glance to me.

"Yes. Yes, you eat them," I tell her, watching in fascination as she stuffs the entire pickle into her mouth. She closes her mouth and chews; then her eyelids flutter. She tilts her head back in a sort of ecstasy that makes me, unexpectedly, blush.

She chews meditatively for a long moment. "Oh, *wow*," she breathes then, exhaling a sigh of bliss. "That was like nothing I've ever had before."

"Really?" I watch, mystified, as she draws another pickle out of the jar.

Maybe she's not from around here. She isn't faking this; I don't think she ever *has* eaten a pickle before. But still...

She can't possibly be an angel.

Can she?

We don't talk much; Gabrielle's too busy devouring the whole jar of pickles and exclaiming over the mound of potato chips that she crunches through in about thirty seconds. And *I'm* too busy staring at the enigmatic woman seated across from me, a woman who claims to be an angel, who'd never eaten—or, apparently, even *seen* – a pickle before today.

It's an odd meal, to say the least.

After finishing my own potato chips, I glance at the clock and realize that, technically, I should be back at the news station in five minutes' time. My lunch break, as improbable and death-defying as it was, is now over. I clear my throat, gathering up my purse and taking out a twenty-dollar bill from my wallet.

"I...um... Sorry, I have to get back to work," I tell Gabrielle, placing the money on the bill that Cheryl gave us. "Thank you for saving my life."

"But I didn't—"

"You did. Thank you." I smile at her softly. "It was...interesting meeting you."

Gabrielle stands, too, with a satisfied smile on her face. "Well, that was delicious. No wonder you venerate the noon hour so much down here," she tells me, her turquoise eyes sparkling.

"Right. Well...good-bye," I tell her, holding tightly to my purse strap as my heart thunders inside of me. Is my heart beating faster because she's standing so close to me?

Do I even have to ask that question?

Gabrielle leans forward then, and I'm not certain what she's about to do until she's taken up my right hand in her own, curling her fingers around my palm as if it's as precious as a gem. She bends down a little, brings my palm up to her mouth, and then she's pressing a warm, soft kiss onto the back of my hand.

I stare at her, my breath coming fast as she flicks her bright, burning gaze to me, looking up at me through her eyelashes. She's still bent at the waist, still pressing a kiss to my hand. She straightens, then, her mouth leaving my skin.

"That's how it's done, isn't it?" she asks me, her lips curving up into a sly smile. "The good-bye-for-now-but-we'll-meet-again kiss? I must've seen it in two dozen of your movies. Oh, the kind without color. I prefer those. Less explodey sounds and car chases."

Despite the overall weirdness, despite the fact that this woman professes to be an angel, and despite the fact that I almost died today, my brain and body are still working just fine. Because as Gabrielle brushed her warm mouth over the back of my hand, every atom of my being woke up in a sudden, vivid way. I'm attracted to her, I know, but when she touched me, the whole world seemed brighter and better. A thrill rocked through me, and it's rocking through me, still.

I feel the blush on my cheeks as Gabrielle reaches up again, this time gliding her hand over my face, feather-light. I shiver at the contact, swallowing.

"You look a bit flushed," she tells me, her smile softening into one of concern. "You weren't injured earlier, were you?"

"No, no," I tell her as she presses her palm against my cheek. There's a roaring in my ears now as I try to calm my heartbeat, as I try to remember how to breathe, how to *speak*. "Um, I'm fine," I protest, and then I take a step back. "I just... It's been an odd day. You know. Anyway, thank you again for everything."

"Don't forget," says Gabrielle, and I pause, perplexed. "You promised Scott a pickle," she tells me with a small smile.

And there, on the table, is an unopened jar of All That and a Bag of Chips-brand pickles.

"Wow," I say, taking up the jar and turning back toward her. "How did you—"

But Gabrielle is already gone.

My eyes dart around the crowded restaurant frantically. But she's not here. She isn't anywhere in sight. And there's nowhere she could have gone, or hidden. The hallway for the restroom is back behind the counter, and the main room of the restaurant itself is large, spacious. The booth is far away from the door...

This isn't possible. Gabrielle just...disappeared.

I hurry back to my office, a million thoughts and feelings warring inside of my head. It's only when I'm standing in front of the news station building that I notice the winged shadow beside me again, vividly black on the pavement.

It's a bright, beautiful day, full of sunshine, not a single cloud in the sky.

I squeeze my eyes shut for a moment and then squint down at the place the shadow occupied on the ground.

But the shadow, like Gabrielle, has vanished, as if it were never really there at all.

And I wonder: did *any* of the events of this afternoon happen? Is Gabrielle even real? Did I just imagine her? Am I losing my mind?

Gripping the jar of pickles in my hands, I draw in a deep, shaky breath and crash through the front doors of BEAN.

The Guardian Angel

Chapter 3: Someone to Watch Over Me

After work, I'm walking down the sidewalk, listening to the next chapter of *Her Heart's Queen* — when I see Gabrielle and instantly press *pause* on my phone's audiobook app. I stare at her, involuntarily, with my mouth hanging open.

What — I mean, how —

My brain short-circuits; my eyes can't believe what they're seeing.

Gabrielle is sitting outside of my apartment building.

She's lounging on the second step of the cement stairs leading up to the front door. Her long legs are crossed at the ankles in front of her, her white sneakers standing out in stark contrast to her tailored black-and-white pinstripe suit, and she's perusing a copy of — appropriately enough — *The National Enquirer*, flipping through the pages with an amused smile.

Confused, I consider the fact that the woman who saved me from death earlier today somehow managed to track me to my place of residence. Did she follow me here? She must have followed me... Has she been following me all day?

Gabrielle lifts her head and regards me with a lingering turquoise gaze, silky brown hair falling over her shoulders; then she flashes me a disarming grin.

I squint up at her, shaking my head, at a loss for words.

"Have you seen this?" She points to the headline on her tabloid copy — *Bigfoot: A Heart as Big as His Feet* — printed beneath a blurry photograph of a Bigfoot-type creature carrying a child out of a burning building. "It's poppycock, of course," she tells me sincerely.

"Poppycock?" I repeat, blinking at her shoes.

"Tell me — do humans really believe this stuff?" She folds up the newspaper and rises, rather regally, to her feet. "Looks more like a hairy fireman who forgot to shave. Still, they've got one thing right," she tells me, thwacking the paper against her leg. "The real Bigfoot is a huge softie. Gave me the shirt off his back — literally — and he hasn't worn a shirt since."

I open my mouth — and then shut it, because no combination of words seems like an adequate response.

Bigfoot is real, she says.

She's an *angel*, she says.

I'm beginning to suspect that I *did* get whipped cream poisoning at the clown convention. Because there's no other explanation for this much...weirdness. And wackiness. Pretty soon, I'll be the subject of a *National Enquirer* article myself.

I pause, frowning as I take stock of the situation. It's clear that Gabrielle has been following me. How else could she have found out where I live? But still...how the hell did she know that I promised Scott a pickle? That question has been nagging at me all afternoon. Did she bug my office and hear our conversation?

Granted, this should all creep me out tremendously, but somehow...it doesn't. It only perplexes me. *She* perplexes me—leaning toward me now with a bright, cheerful smile, a smile that becomes a little sly when her turquoise gaze flicks to mine. And just like that, I'm blushing from head to toe.

She's so self-assured, standing before me as if we're old friends, as if she hasn't got a care in the world, as if we're meant to be right here, right now, and all's right with the world.

There's something about this woman— this impossible, confusing, beautiful woman— that makes my heart skip a beat. Ironic, because I have never, in all of my life, taken that phrase seriously before. Your heart *literally* skips a beat? Doesn't that sound, well, dangerous?

But I don't feel any danger as I stare up at Gabrielle, heart stuttering inside of my chest. I only feel kind of warm and flustered and bewildered.

And, inexplicably, safe.

I clear my throat.

Gabrielle tilts her head at me.

"Look," I begin haltingly. "I'm...not convinced of this whole..." I shake my head, sigh. "This whole guardian angel thing," I force out, crossing my arms in front of me—which, I realize, probably makes me look obstinate, even sullen. I let my arms fall loosely to my sides, sighing again.

"We-e-e-ll," says Gabrielle, drawing out the word as she places her copy of the *Enquirer* beneath her arm and shoves her hands into her pockets. She frowns. "I suppose I could think of a way to prove it to you—the 'whole guardian angel thing,' as you put it. Want to hop inside?" she asks me, angling her head toward my apartment building.

"I..." I lick my lips thoughtfully. "I don't know if that's such a good idea. I mean, it isn't that I don't trust you, but... This is all just so—"

"Weird and wacky?"

My mouth falls open.

"All right, then." Gabrielle's turquoise eyes flash brightly. "Your eight-year-old birthday party," she says, her mouth twitching at the corners. "There was purple everywhere—purple streamers, purple paper plates, purple roses on your cake. And there were pitchers and pitchers of grape Kool-Aid. You drank so much that day that you got sick and never drank Kool-Aid again, even though it was your favorite. Um—what else? Oh! You had a unicorn pinata that you nicknamed Sparkles before you bludgeoned it to pieces. Apparently, you liked candy quite a bit more than you liked poor Sparkles."

I pale. "Well, that's...a lucky guess. What child of the eighties *wouldn't* have a unicorn pinata at her birthday party?" I ask, drawing in a deep breath. "And purple is the best color—"

"You got a My Little Pony, Applejack, as a gift from your parents," says Gabrielle determinedly. "And your little brother scribbled all over it with markers that night, because he was jealous that you had a party. He had chicken pox during his birthday and couldn't have a party." She raises her brows wonderingly. "You humans are fond of your parties, aren't you?" she says, smiling.

I gape at her, stunned to silence. I couldn't feel more shocked if I'd just seen a ghost. I'm so rattled, in fact, that my hands are shaking; I glance down at my phone, clutched in my fingers, worried that I might drop it.

"*Now* will you let me in?" asks Gabrielle innocently.

I'm still staring at her, still speechless, so Gabrielle takes my silence as a *no*.

"Okay. How about..." She looks up

toward the sky, eyes closed, and then returns her gaze to me. "Your bedroom when you were fifteen," she says, tilting her head to the side and smiling again. "It was plastered with posters of Diane Sawyer. You drank seven cups of coffee every day that you were in college, trying to juggle your schoolwork along with your internship at the local public access station...where you reported on college sports scores and drunken UFO call-ins. There were," she says, chuckling, "a *lot* of drunken UFO call-ins. And many of them were valid, though you'd never guess it, considering the less-than-credible witnesses."

I blink at her, breathing fast. "How in the *world* do you know all of this?" I whisper.

Gabrielle smiles warmly at me. "I know *you*," she says.

"Oh." For a short, still moment, I watch her, flummoxed—and mesmerized. Then, "Yes," I say, my voice soft, wispy. I shake my head, brushing a strand of hair out of my eyes. "Yeah. Come on in." The invitation surprises me, even as I make it, because I can't believe I'm letting a stranger who believes she's an angel into my apartment...

But how else could she have known those things about me? I could chalk some of it up to the possibility of her stalking me, sure. But only my brother and I knew about Applejack. He stole her from me after the party, hiding in his bedroom until he'd scribbled all over her orange-colored body with black marker. And then when he showed his handiwork to me, he got scared, realizing how much trouble he'd get into when our parents found out, so he made me promise not to tell. In exchange for my silence, he traded me his most prized G.I. Joe action figure—which I loved even more than I would have loved the pony. I dressed the action figure up in some of my Skipper doll's clothes and painted his face with makeup until Joe became Barbara Jones, G.I. Jane...*my* most prized possession.

I never told my parents—or anyone. Only my brother and I knew about Applejack's fate.

But somehow Gabrielle knows, too.

When we walk up the stairs and into my apartment, Sawyer glances toward us from her couch-potato spot and blinks her puppy dog eyes.

Usually, Sawyer greets me with a mildly enthusiastic series of tail wags—until I grab her leash. Then she begrudgingly eases herself off of the couch, waddling over to me with a sigh, as if to say, "Fine, let's go for a walk, but I don't particularly want to be doing this...just so you know."

Today? Today Sawyer does something that I haven't seen her do since she was a much younger dog. She *bounds* off of the sofa, trotting over to us with a tail that's wagging so furiously, it's a fluffy brown-and-white blur. None of this enthusiasm, by the way, is for me. Sawyer makes a beeline for Gabrielle, and then she's shoving her long collie nose under Gabrielle's right hand, forcing the woman to pet her.

Which Gabrielle does, sinking down into a crouch and laughing warmly as Sawyer bathes her face with doggy kisses.

"Sawyer, be good. I'm sorry. She's isn't usually like this. I can't remember a time I've seen her so enthusiastic," I say, but Gabrielle waves off my apology with a good-natured smile, rising from her crouch as she ruffles the fur behind Sawyer's ears.

"She's a very sweet dog," says Gabrielle fondly. "It was wonderful of you to adopt her, you know. Out of all of the dogs at that shelter, you chose the one who had been hit by a car. Not a lot of people would have done the same."

I meet her turquoise gaze, my heartbeat thundering in my ears. "How did you—"

"You still don't believe me, do you?" asks Gabrielle, her eyes bright with intensity.

"I'm trying, but..." I wrap my arms around myself, drawing in a deep breath. "It's a lot to digest. This isn't part of my worldview. This isn't... I don't..." I gesture uselessly, searching for the right words. "Gabrielle, you think you're an angel. And I don't *believe* in angels."

"A lot of people don't believe in things that are real," she says, raising an eyebrow. "Belief has absolutely nothing to do with whether something exists or not. Consider the moon landing."

"The moon landing," I repeat incredulously.

"Do you *know* how many humans believe that the moon landing was faked?"

I shake my head. "There are conspiracy theorists—"

"And their theories are wrong. I promise you, your people landed on the moon. A few centuries later than that race from the next galaxy over, but, hey, at least you made it there eventually!"

"That race from the next galaxy over," I murmur, sinking down on my couch because my legs are suddenly too weak to hold me up. "Now you're talking about aliens," I say flatly.

"Let me guess." She regards me curiously, one hand on her hip. "You don't believe in aliens, either."

"Um..." I begin, but then Gabrielle is seated in my favorite comfy chair, across from me on the couch.

"Ah, what's this?" She leans forward, her eyes alight, and picks up a thick hardcover book from the coffee table. She begins to thumb through it, smiling hugely as she glances down at the full-color pictures—because it's a book about *angels*, full of the old, classical paintings of wings and halos and glowing beings descending from the heavens...

She points to an image of a winged woman in a lavender robe with a finger crooked toward the sky. "I don't know where your artists came up with the whole angels-in-robes thing. We angels have impeccable fashion sense, you know." She smooths the lapels of her jacket and grins at me. "You'd no sooner see us in shapeless robes than you would in clown costumes. Well, unless the situation called for an extreme fashion faux pas, of course."

I rise, paling, and—gently—I take the book out of Gabrielle's hands. She glances up at me in surprise, but I press the book to my stomach and shake my head.

"Sorry, I don't mean to be rude, but..." I swallow; my face is burning. "This book was Melinda's—"

"Oh, right," says Gabrielle, leaning back in the chair and putting her hands behind her head. She lifts a single eyebrow as she murmurs, "Melinda. The old *squeeze*."

I stare at her, stricken, and feel my hot skin grow cold. "Have you been following me for my entire life?" I whisper, holding the book even tighter.

Gabrielle's gaze flicks to mine, and she lowers her hands into her lap. "No," she tells me, and she sounds sincere. "Only lately. But I have access to all of your memories now, since they might prove to be useful information during my guardianship." She stands up; we're only inches apart. I realize how close she's standing to me at the same moment that she does. Her smile deepens as she searches my face, long lashes lowered, but then the brightness of her turquoise eyes dims slightly as she glances away. "People are only assigned guardian angels when they really need them."

"Oh." I bite my lower lip, take a step back, and replace the angel book on the coffee table. "Not that I believe you," I tell her, trying my best to sound neutral rather than antagonistic, "but why do I *need* a guardian angel?"

Gabrielle, still focused on some distant point or far-off memory, shakes her head, says, "I shouldn't say." Her brow furrows. "Honestly, I'm not quite sure myself." She shrugs a little, raking a hand through her hair before she folds back down and sits in the chair. "It's all very *vague* and *secretive*, you know," she says, eyes wide and achingly blue. "I only know that I'm here to protect you."

I fall back onto the couch, breathing deeply. We stare at one another for a long moment while I work up the courage to say, in an unnaturally high voice, "Protect me from...what?"

Gabrielle leans back, legs splayed in front

of her. She looks perfectly at ease, in her element, despite the fact that we hardly know one another. But I guess I'm not a stranger to her, am I?

The thought is dizzying, disconcerting.

"Well, I figured I was meant to rescue you from that almost-car accident, but that wasn't it, obviously, because I'm still here." She taps her chest with her index finger and sighs. "I mean, you could be in danger at anytime, considering your line of work and the news stories you've been assigned to cover." She muses for a moment, hand to her chin. "You could be attacked by angry chihuahuas, angry tots in tiaras, angry birds. Saw a movie about that once. Put me off birds for decades." She shudders. "But the danger could be something as unpredictable as, oh, paper airplanes flying every which way. They're quite pointy, you know."

"I'm sorry," I finally tell her, spreading my hands in my lap. "It's not that I don't *want* to believe you," I say, which I'm surprised I'm admitting to her, but it's true. I almost *do* want to believe her. But this defies science, logic. Common sense. It just...seems impossible. Angels. *Real* angels.

I stammer, "It's just...this is all so hard to..." I drift off, frowning.

Gabrielle shrugs again, standing smoothly. I think, for a moment, that she's going to excuse herself from my presence and leave, but that's not what she does at all.

"Right, then. Time to bring out the big guns," says Gabrielle with a wide smile. "Oh, not literally," she adds, unbuttoning the front of her suit jacket and straightening her sleeves. "All angels take a vow of nonviolence. Anyway...imagine a drum roll, please."

And then...

Feathers. Long white feathers that shimmer and shine. Feathers that seem to glow from within, like each long, plumed object is a miniature sun. Feathers that are attached to magnificent, massive wings that rise around the both of us. Huge. These wings are *huge*.

Gabrielle shifts her shoulders, her wings stretching overhead and then smoothly folding against her back as she beams at me. Her wings glow. In that moment, *she* glows, glows like a radiant thing, like she's made of stars.

I stare at her, hyperventilating, blood thundering in my veins. It's thundering so fast, so hard, in fact, that there are black spots marring my vision.

"Don't faint," Gabrielle sighs, as I faint.

⏳

I wake up in my bed on my back, staring at the ceiling with bleary eyes, the late evening sunshine reflecting off of my sheer curtains and playing across the ceiling in pretty, golden bars.

I take a deep breath, rise up onto my elbows, and peer down at myself, perplexed. I'm still wearing my work clothes, and I'm lying on top of my comforter, the thin belt buckle of my skirt pinching my stomach, my blouse untucked a little from the waistline. I'm still wearing my flats, too, my feet dangling off the edge of the bed.

I'm not normally a nap person, but I must have been so tired when I got home from work that I sprawled out on the bed for a moment of rest. I must have accidentally fallen asleep.

I sigh out, flop back down, and point my gaze toward the ceiling again, rubbing the back of my head as I yawn. Yeah. That's it. I fell asleep, and I had a really weird dream about an angel hanging out in my living room.

I shut my eyes for a moment, remembering the vividness of her wings, how they shimmered in the sunshine streaming through the windows. The feathers were so fine and elegant, and the wings themselves were large and soft-looking, *beautiful...*

It makes sense that I would have a dream like that. Because—let's be honest—Gabrielle is kind of my *dream* woman, crazy angel thing notwithstanding.

I lie still, considering the weight of this realization. Gabrielle is funny. I have a thing for funny women. She's kind. Who doesn't want a partner who's kind?

She loves potato chips and funky restaurants as much as me...

And Sawyer is crazy about her.

It's a shame, then, that she isn't real. Because I must have dreamed all of it—the near-accident, the deli, the wings. She's only a phantom of my imagination. But...I'm kind of high-fiving my imagination right now, because Gabrielle is one of my best inventions. She's...amazing. Like, *utterly* amazing, the kind of amazing I didn't realize I'd been waiting for my entire life...but apparently, I had.

I stretch, yawn again.

But then I stiffen, fingers brushing against the Band-Aid on my forehead.

Hmm.

I don't remember putting a Band-Aid on my forehead.

I look around, confused, and then I stare at the steaming mug of tea on my nightstand, a tea bag bobbing on its surface.

And, oddly enough, there's the distinctive smell of burning food in the air...

Suddenly anxious, I clear my throat. I feel ridiculous, like I'm talking to a figment of my imagination, but I call out tentatively, into the quiet of my apartment, "Gabrielle?"

Silence is my only reply.

I sigh, slump against the mattress,

chastising myself. Well, I can be kind of forgetful sometimes. I must have made myself this cup of tea and then fallen asleep, only for a moment... So I guess my Gabrielle dream was, in actuality, a very short dream, though it didn't feel short at all.

Maybe I stuck the Band-aid on over a cut... Did I have a cut on my forehead? My mind grapples with time and reality, trying to piece things together in a way that makes sense...

But then Gabrielle pokes her head through the doorway, smiling, and my tenuous grasp on time and reality evaporates.

I stare at her, heart pounding, as I sit up, leaning back on my hands to steady myself.

Beneath the golden halo of an almost-sunset, red highlights gleam among her satiny brown strands. The sunshine reflects, too, off of her turquoise eyes, illuminating them as if from within.

I remember the wings, the feathers. I remember that Gabrielle herself glowed, and my heart begins to beat a little faster.

Is it possible?

Is she really here? Is she really...an angel?

"How's the tea?" she asks me, pushing off from the door frame and stepping into the room. "Hope you don't mind, but I made myself a grilled cheese sandwich. Real one this time, no potato chips. Well, I *tried* to make a grilled cheese sandwich..." She frowns mildly as she holds up a small plate bearing the charred remains of something that looks vaguely sandwich-shaped. It's so black that when Gabrielle lifts the sandwich-shape thing up with a forefinger, flecks of ash fall from the sides of it. She curls her hand around the sandwich, lifts it to her lips, and—as I stare in horror—she takes a bite of it.

"Mm. Tastes a bit like Pompeii," says Gabrielle with a wry smile, crunching on her bite of charcoal.

I don't know if I'm hysterical, incredulous, or actually amused, but suddenly I start to laugh—uncontrollably. Hiccuping and breathless. Gabrielle flicks her gaze to me, and then she's laughing, too, the warm peals of her laughter filling my bedroom in much the same way that the last rays of sunshine are. Gabrielle moves into the room gracefully and sits down next to me on the bed, crossing her legs as she holds out her plate.

"Fancy a bite?" she asks me, her mouth curving up.

I only laugh harder.

Finally, after I've laughed myself sore, I draw in a deep, bewildered breath, and that's when I notice how close Gabrielle is to me. Her face is turned toward mine, her lips smiling warmly, her eyes bright and oh-so-beautiful that they make my heart flip-flop in my chest.

I gulp down more air as a question fills me, a question that I really, *really* wish I knew the answer to, a surprising question that I can't believe I'm thinking about.

Do angels kiss? I wonder.

For a long moment, I search her bright turquoise eyes. Her impossibly turquoise eyes.

And I wonder something else: *Can angels be...gay?*

I never went to Sunday School, and I've never given angels a second thought. Melinda was into New Agey stuff like crystals and chakras and guardian angels, but she knew I wasn't interested in spirituality — which was one of the reasons she left me, or so she claimed in her after-breakup text. You know, her after-cheating text, where she blamed me for the fact that we "fell apart as a couple."

I swallow and lick my lips, thoughts of Melinda weighing heavily upon me as I look at Gabrielle, as I wonder about her, wonder how any of this is possible... I have no religious foundation to fall back on, to build upon, but even if I did, I have a feeling that Gabrielle would tell me that most humans' conceptions of angels is far off the mark.

She's gazing at me so softly, almost reverently, and my heart accelerates as I realize that there's a fire burning in her too-blue eyes.

I...don't know what's gotten into me. I hit my head when I fainted after Gabrielle unfurled her wings—but I don't think I can blame my current state on a fall. I find myself leaning toward Gabrielle now, and she leans toward me, too.

I close my eyes, my breath coming too fast. And I feel Gabrielle's mouth...but it isn't pressed to my mouth. The angel—because I think I believe her now; what choice do I have?—plants a soft kiss on my cheek, just beside my lips.

She remains there for a long moment, her cheek against mine, her warm breath moving my hair, before she shifts, bringing her mouth to my ear.

I shiver as she whispers: "Want to watch a Lifetime movie and eat Ben & Jerry's?"

It's so unexpected that I laugh, tension broken. And then I'm nodding, my heart still pounding in response to the sudden contact, to her kiss against my cheek. Gabrielle slides off the bed, standing and offering her hands to me with a small smile. I slip my fingers between hers, and she helps me stand up.

There's a moment of panic when I go to my freezer and realize that, as impossible as this sounds, I'm *out* of ice cream. I stare at the bag of frozen peas and the empty ice cube tray with a frown.

"It's not a tragedy," Gabrielle tells me with an easy shrug and smile, peering over my shoulder at the nearly empty freezer compartment. "Let's walk to the corner store and pick up some ice cream, hmm?"

I hold onto the freezer door handle for a moment, realizing how very...odd all of this is. Okay, "odd" doesn't even begin to cover it. I'm going to walk to the corner store with an angel? To buy ice cream? This is my life now?

I guess that somewhere between telling me about a graffitied My Little Pony she could never have known about and being shown impossible, enormous, shimmering wings, I suspended my disbelief. I've begun to accept that Gabrielle is, in fact, an angel.

My *guardian* angel.

So, apparently, this *is* my life now. I grab my purse, and Gabrielle picks up Sawyer's leash, flashing me a small smile.

Every time *I* pick up Sawyer's leash, my collie rolls her eyes, as if to say, "I have better things planned for the evening than a *walk*. Thanks, but no thanks." But when Gabrielle picks up the leash, this is not how Sawyer reacts. She grins, leaps up, and trots over. I stare, astonished. Sawyer *never* trots, because her hips bother her so much. Like Gabrielle said, Sawyer was hit by a car before I adopted her, and the bone that the vet had to piece back together in her leg always gives her grief when she moves faster than a snail.

"I don't think I've ever seen her move so quickly," I murmur, a little mystified, as

Gabrielle leans over and clips Sawyer's collar to her leash. I try not to stare at Gabrielle's rear as she's bent over—and I utterly fail; I mean, it's gorgeous, glorious—but then the angel straightens and smiles slyly at me.

"Well, you see..." She trails off, runs a hand through her hair as if she's almost chagrined. "I did a little something to help with that. With Sawyer."

I blink at her. "What do you mean?"

"Angels can, under some circumstances, offer a bit of their power in exchange for a healing or a little...um, I guess you could call it 'good luck,'" she tells me, glancing down at Sawyer with unabashed affection. "And poor Sawyer didn't deserve to be hit by that car. Her angel at the time was brand new, inexperienced, so she didn't save her wholly. But she did keep the car driver from taking her life, so I can't fault her for it."

I stare at Gabrielle, my mouth turning up at the corners. "Wait a second. Animals are assigned angels, too?"

Gabrielle regards me with a did-you-really-just-ask-me-that expression, as if I just wondered aloud whether salt water is, in fact, salty. "Of *course* they do!" she tells me with a wide smile. "You're all so important. Every living creature on this planet is so very important." She intones this last sentence like a prayer as she holds my gaze, her eyes large, glittering with emotion. "Every life has consequence, is worthy, precious..." She shakes her head, looks away as she bites her lip. "The problem is that none of you truly knows how precious you are," she whispers, scratching gently behind Sawyer's ears. "If you did, most of the problems you face would—*poof*—disappear."

My breath catches in my throat, and I let it out in a long sigh as Gabrielle hands me Sawyer's leash. When Gabrielle's hand presses the leash into my palm, she lingers there for a moment, her warm skin against mine.

"I helped heal Sawyer because it was easy, Erin," says Gabrielle then, as if she can sense the questions brewing in my mind. "She was partially crippled because the bone healed incorrectly. I just realigned it. It was a small thing, just a tiny movement, really, but angels cannot do major adjustments. We don't have that power, and large interferences alter too much. Healing a human of anything more than a minor injury is beyond us, and changing the fact of whether someone lived or died... Well, that's *far* beyond us." She searches my gaze. "We all do the best we can," she murmurs.

Mystified, I nod; we leave my apartment with Sawyer. I shut the door behind us, and we walk down the hallway together, so close we're almost touching.

There's something crackling between us

now, though I don't think I could define it, exactly. I'm attracted to Gabrielle—very attracted—and I was right, when I was sitting in bed, considering what I'd thought had been a "dream." Gabrielle truly is my dream woman. But as we move down the hallway, aiming for the staircase, it strikes me that there's something else going on here, a feeling that stretches between us, as if we're somehow connected...though I could never tell you by what. It's warm, this feeling, and soft. Feather-soft.

I guess I could chalk it up to the fact that Gabrielle's my guardian angel. An angel connection. That must be it.

But even as I think that thought, my heart rebels against it.

What if it's because there's truly something special between the two of you? Something you can't explain, but that's there, all the same? my heart wonders.

But that's ridiculous, of course, and I chuckle quietly to myself as we take the steps. I don't believe in stuff like this; it's woo-woo and far out of my comfort zone...

But aren't angels out of your comfort zone, too? my heart insists. *And yet you're standing next to one.*

I push that thought out of my head and heart as we descend the staircase and exit my building, stepping into the setting sunlight of a warm summer evening. I take a deep breath, inhaling the heavy green of the trees, the scent of rain in the clouds that will eventually open tonight, washing the whole city in a cleansing downpour.

"Shall we?" asks Gabrielle. She offers me her arm, like she's a still out of an old movie, and grins playfully at me.

I thread my arm through hers, my heartbeat hammering as she presses her arm to her side; my elbow is nestled in the crook between her ribs and her breast. My breathing comes a little faster as we turn and begin to walk up the block, Sawyer ambling happily ahead of us.

We reach the corner store quickly. A little too quickly. I was enjoying our old-fashioned stroll, arm in arm, collie pacing ahead of us, interested in everything, finding a hundred smelly spots to sniff, instead of waddling as usual, wishing she were back home on her couch again.

It was a no-brainer when I chose Sawyer so many years ago. I've always been a big softie for animals with sob stories, but there was more to it than that. The moment that I went into the shelter and saw Sawyer looking at me through the wire mesh fencing, my heart seemed to pour out of my body and surround her with so much love that I didn't even need to officially "meet" her, though I did, scratching her behind her ears as if I knew, instinctively, exactly where her special spot was. And I guess I did, because the minute I rubbed the place behind her floppy brown ears, Sawyer started to kick her back leg, eyes closed in pleasure as her foot thumped against the floor.

The volunteers at the shelter told me about the car accident; they told me that Sawyer should probably have weight kept off of her, that she needed to stay on the skinny side, because more weight would make it much harder for her to move about in life. Then I brought her home, and she was the best dog I could ever imagine, and I loved her utterly, wholeheartedly. So, of course, because I loved her so much, I bought her cuts of meat (hilarious, the vegetarian ordering cuts of ham and beef at the counter for her dog, but I did it happily, because *I love my dog*), feeding her the best diet I could cobble together from the internet (and with a lot of helpful input from my vet). In the end, Sawyer put on a little bit of weight, and her joints and hips started hurting a little more.

But now? Now, I'm seeing in front of me the dog that Sawyer would have been if that car had never hit her. And I'm choked up with emotion because of it, because seeing her so joyful and engaged and pain-free makes tears spring to my eyes.

An angel did this. The angel holding my

arm. The angel who saved my life earlier today.

It's weird. All of this is very weird.

But it's also very wonderful.

"What flavor?" asks Gabrielle, when we reach the convenience store.

"Flavor?" I ask her, the question bringing me back to reality with a jolt. "Oh, ice cream, right," I tell her with an embarrassed shake of my head. "Uh...what do you want to try?"

"All of them?" says Gabrielle hopefully, and I laugh.

"Hey..." I ask her then, wondering. "Have you ever *had* ice cream before?"

Gabrielle shakes her head, her mouth turned up at the corners. "Before this afternoon," she tells me, leaning a little closer, as if she's conspiring with me, "I'd never had any food at all. The potato chips were my first introduction to Earth food."

"Your *first*?" I stare at her. "If I'd known, I would've suggested something, I don't know, classier or—"

"It was a *great* introduction," Gabrielle assures me, her voice a low purr. And then she steps away, sliding her arm out of mine. "I'll be right back," she tells me, walking toward the entrance to the convenience store, a threshold that Sawyer, unfortunately, can't cross. I'll have to wait outside with her.

"Wait," I tell Gabrielle, pulling my purse off of my shoulder and rummaging around inside of it. "You need money." I hold up my wallet, but she's shaking her head, smiling mysteriously as she shoves her hands into her suit jacket's pockets.

"Nah," she tells me. And then, still wearing that mysterious smile, she ducks inside of the store.

"Well," I tell Sawyer, and I sink down onto the curb to sit next to her. My collie companionably leans against my shoulder, giving me one lick on my nose, then sighing in contentment. "It's been a strange day, huh, baby girl?" I ask her, ruffling her ears and staring at the empty city street, awash in the golden sunshine of sunset, storm clouds lingering around the horizon biding their time.

Gabrielle exits the convenience store a minute later, juggling four plastic bags full of Ben & Jerry's pints. "I bought them out," she tells me, with a bit of a sheepish grin. "Because running out of ice cream is a hardship that I think you need to avoid. You know, it's one of my duties as your guardian angel, to ensure that you avoid tragedies."

"But...you're an angel!" I tell her, standing up and dusting off my bottom. "How could you possibly have paid for those? Do angels have money?" I chuckle weakly.

"Oh, we get some of your Earth money for assignments," says Gabrielle, with a shrug. She juggles her bags, and then she's pulling an enormous wad of cash out of her pocket. I stare at it, disbelieving. I've never seen so much paper money in my life. "We're advised to spend it wisely, and I figured this was spending it *very* wisely," says Gabrielle, nodding to her bags.

I laugh, shaking my head, and then we're walking back toward my apartment, as I worry that I won't be able to fit that many cartons of ice cream in my freezer.

Turns out that, because my freezer is so empty, the ice cream fits perfectly. There is, in fact, the *exact* amount of room needed, and there were a *lot* of pints of ice cream, which makes me a little suspicious that Gabrielle used some of her angelic powers to give me extra freezer space.

She said she could do *little* things. Perhaps adding space to my freezer qualifies as a little thing.

Since we've settled in for the night, I give Gabrielle some of my pajamas to wear, and she looks oddly adorable in orange PJs decorated with blue kittens. The pajama top is a little snug, stretching across her broad shoulders — and I'm assuming that angels need broad shoulders for their wings. Honestly, I'm trying not to concentrate on all of the things that I find attractive about Gabrielle, but my eyes keep being drawn, of their own accord, to her muscled shoulders and upper arms.

I fry up two grilled cheese sandwiches — and they're both a little burned, but not as blackened as Gabrielle's earlier attempt—and we eat them companionably together, sitting on my couch shoulder to shoulder as we laugh at a ridiculously scandalous Lifetime movie together.

The movie is *incredibly* ridiculous, which, normally, I love, but for some reason, the cinematic atrocity just isn't holding my attention tonight. As we sit side by side, I'm amazed to realize exactly how comfortable I am with Gabrielle. I mean, it's partially due to the fact that she's laughing at the same parts of the movie that make me laugh (the acting on this one is spectacularly bad, adding to its charm), coupled with the fact that Melinda and I rarely watched television together, let alone awful Lifetime movies; our tastes in everything were just too different.

Honestly? Right now, I feel like *I'm* in a particularly odd Lifetime movie. I mean, who lets a stranger into their house and life like this, especially one who claims to be a *paranormal being*? But there's something so innately trustworthy about Gabrielle...and she *does* have wings. I saw the wings. I believe now, wholly and utterly, that Gabrielle is exactly who she says she is.

Really, though, I know it's more than that. The corner of my mouth, where my mouth meets my cheek, still faintly tingles where Gabrielle placed her frustratingly chaste kiss on me.

God, I'm so confused. And so smitten.

After the movie, we both stand up, stretching. We ate a pint of ice cream each, dipping spoons into about ten others to taste-test them, and I start to put the unfinished pints back into the freezer.

"I have an air mattress I can inflate for you," I tell Gabrielle over my shoulder, shutting the freezer door. "It's not *great*. I mean, it isn't the most comfortable thing, but it certainly beats sleeping on the couch—"

"Oh, that won't be necessary," she tells me with another one of her disarming smiles. She shrugs and stretches again. "I don't need to sleep. I have to keep watch, you know, in case of..." She stops for a moment, thinking. "Hmm. I can't imagine what might attack you here in the middle of the night, sound asleep in your bed, but...just in *case*." She sits back down on the couch and picks up the angel book from the coffee table, placing it on her lap.

"Oh, yeah, the whole...guardian thing," I say uncertainly. And a bit lamely. I stand in the doorway between the living room and kitchen and clear my throat with a small shrug. "Well, good night, Gabrielle."

Gabrielle flicks her turquoise gaze up to me, her smile gentle. "Good night, Erin," she says, her voice softening on my name.

My knees are a little weak as I turn and walk back down the hallway, toward the bathroom. While I brush my teeth, wash my face, perform my nightly routine, I think about the way that Gabrielle looked at me, her blue eyes gentle and burning at the same time.

So I go to bed, and — unsurprisingly — I have a difficult time falling asleep.

My mind plays back, over and over, the strangest day I've ever had. I think about Gabrielle rising over me after she saved me from being hit by a car. I think of Gabrielle's smile...

And behind my closed eyes, I keep seeing Gabrielle's beautiful wings.

The Guardian Angel

Chapter 4: Personally Involved

Over the next week, Gabrielle becomes a strange but comfortable fixture in my life. We have breakfast, lunch and dinner together every day, Gabrielle meeting up with me at All That and a Bag of Chips during my lunch breaks because she has to, and I quote, "try every flavor of potato chips this fine establishment has to offer." Since the deli boasts that they can make over a thousand different flavor combinations, I'm wondering exactly how long Gabrielle expects her angel guardianship to last.

And I'm highly aware, every moment I'm in Gabrielle's company, that our relationship looks, at least from the outside, as if we're dating. I wake up in the morning to a glass of orange juice on the kitchen table, an angel seated next to me, smiling over her own cup of tea. We talk about our plans for the day, any funny/weird/bad dreams I had the night before, which Lifetime movies we'd like to watch that evening. And then, when I come home from work, we curl up on the couch together, laughing as we dip our spoons into one another's ice cream containers, delighting in terrible movie after terrible movie...

Isn't that kind of the textbook definition of dating? Growing closer moment by moment, sharing laughter, spending all of your spare time together, and when you're apart, counting the minutes until you'll be together again...

Okay, maybe that last one is just me. And, in truth, we're never actually apart. Gabrielle is always nearby, I know. Though I can't see her when I'm at the station, I can feel her—a warm, soothing presence watching over me.

The fact of the matter is we're *aren't* really dating, and that makes things a little, well, awkward, from my point of view. Ever since the not-really-a-kiss kiss that Gabrielle gave me, placing her soft mouth against my cheek, her breath warm against my skin...I've got to confess: I've been aching for a *real* kiss from her.

I don't know why she kissed me so chastely that afternoon. Her eyes had been burning with something that I'd read as desire, but maybe I had read her expression incorrectly. She's an angel, after all, not a human. Maybe cheek kisses are how angels show affection to one other. Regardless, Gabrielle hasn't given me any other indication that she might be interested in me romantically, not a hint.

Just...nothing.

Sometimes she teases me, sure, her turquoise eyes flashing, her mouth turning up at the corners wryly...but she remains—*maddeningly*—physically aloof. Granted, she's offered her arm to me a few times, but I chalk that up to manners, politeness, and the fact that, apparently, she's watched a lot of black-and-white movies.

I just don't know what to think, how to make sense of her presence in my life—or what to do about all of these feelings she's provoked inside of me. I have so many questions, an infinity of questions. Gabrielle never talks about herself at all, about other angels or where she resided before she began her guardianship of me (in the clouds? In heaven?). She's never talked to me about what it's like to be a guardian angel—how long she's been doing it, if she's ever done anything else.... She's a complete mystery, a mystery that I'm desperate to solve.

Today is, blessedly, Friday, and I'm killing time at work daydreaming about Gabrielle, wondering about her...and adding rubber bands to Scott's head-size rubber band ball.

The giant thing is Scott's pride and joy; it's been accumulating girth for weeks now. He adds a couple of rubber bands to the growing sphere every time we get sent out to cover a new, ridiculous fluff piece. And we've been covering a *lot* of ridiculous fluff pieces lately.

At this rate, the rubber band ball is going to be too heavy to lift by the end of the month.

"McEvoy!" one of the techs bellows, sticking his head around the door frame and into the office. His name is Brian, and he hates his job as much as the rest of us do. According to Scott, the loathing he has for his job is to blame for Brian's bad attitude. He frowns when he sees me, as if I'm inconveniencing him somehow, as if he wasn't just calling my name. He takes his phone out, grimaces when he glances at the screen, and slides it back into his pocket. "We just got a tip that a chimpanzee escaped from the Franklin Park Zoo," he tells me, frown deepening. Somehow, his whole *body* looks like it's frowning now. "Wanna cover it? You're the only reporter available."

I glance at the clock, then silently curse. I'm the only reporter available because, in my distraction, I forgot to take my lunch break, and everyone else is out on theirs. Missing my lunch break means missing an opportunity to hang out with Gabrielle.

Focus, Erin. I chew on my lower lip, considering the story; then I nod, standing up. An escaped chimpanzee, as crazy as it sounds, is the most legitimate news story I've been assigned to cover in a very long time. Longer than I'd care to admit.

"Sure, we can take it. Let me just grab Scott," I tell him, and Brian nods, turning to go.

"I've sent him the coordinates on his phone," he tells me over his shoulder. Then he brushes past Scott, who's coming back into the room, laden down with bags of chips and cans of cola from the vending machine.

"What's up?" Scott asks me, as I pick up his camera.

"We've got a story. A chimp escaped from the zoo," I tell him, and he reacts in much the same way I did: positively.

"Hey, we might be moving up in the world, partner," he says with a wink, grabbing his equipment case.

"Infinitesimally." I chuckle. "Anyway, Brian told me the only reason we're getting the gig is because everyone else is out on lunch. But, hey, it's mildly exciting, isn't it? Almost-real news!" I smile brightly.

"I'll take it," Scott tells me. "Mildly exciting is better than bone-numbingly boring."

"My thoughts exactly."

Together, we trot out of the building and climb into the news van, openly psyched for the opportunity.

"Here." Scott hands me his phone. "Where are we headed?"

I peer down at the screen, scrolling through the information that Brian texted us. "Okay, so, the chimp was last sighted on the outskirts of the northern area of Franklin Park," I tell Scott, reading off of his phone. "Is that too vague?"

"Yeah, but we'll do our best, like always,"

he tells me, flooring the gas pedal as he veers out into oncoming traffic.

Though Gabrielle has been with me every morning, every night, and my companion during every lunch break, she gives me my privacy during the workday — or, rather, she isn't visible to me. Sometimes I catch her shadow on the station's walls when I'm walking down the corridors, and I once saw her shadow lingering just beside my desk. As we speed down the streets toward Franklin Park now, I can see a shadow racing alongside the van's shadow: a large shadow with wings, far too large and, well, human-shaped to be a bird.

I smile to myself, tapping my fingers against the glass.

I feel safe. I know that's how guardian angels are supposed to make you feel — at least, according to pop culture wisdom. There's more to it than that, though. Gabrielle takes her mission to protect me seriously, but she's also there for me in a different, deeper sense. I don't claim to know how angelic missions work, but I'm pretty sure she wasn't obligated by angelic law to buy me all of those pints of ice cream, and I'm about 99.99% positive that she is not required to watch cheesy movies ad nauseum with her guardee.

As Scott pulls our van into a space near the park, I groan, dragging myself out of yet another pleasant daydream about Gabrielle.

There are already a ton of other news vans close by. We're probably the last to arrive, I realize, as I read the call letters on the sides of the vehicles. All of the major news stations are here, along with a handful of not-so-major ones, including a reporter for the public access station LEM, BEAN's rival in pathetic, single-digit viewership.

There are reporters and cameramen setting up outside, the reporters doing soundchecks into their microphones, the cameramen checking their equipment and getting plugged into their networks. The park itself is big, but most of the reporters are stationed front and center before the walls of the Franklin Park Zoo so that they can, at least, get a shot of the zoo in the background as they cover their story. So many reporters are gathered in the same area that it's a bit overcrowded; still, they all seem to want the shot with the walls of the zoo behind them.

As I open the van door and scan the area, I pause and blink, heart skipping a beat.

Because there's Gabrielle, leaning against one of the distant trees, her arms crossed over her chest. I recognize her immediately because she's wearing her familiar bright white sneakers and her black-and-white pinstripe suit. What's she doing here? More importantly, why is she suddenly visible to me?

I swallow, my mouth suddenly dry.

Is something wrong? Is something

terrible going to happen? Is today the day?

The flipside to having a really gorgeous angel protecting you is realizing that something awful is bound to happen to you sooner or later. That she's only here because you need protection from some unknown, unimagined danger—looming in the future like a silent thundercloud poised over your head.

"Get the camera going, okay?" I ask Scott distractedly as I lick my lips, eyes glued to the tree. "I'll...I'll be right back."

"Sure," he replies quizzically, shrugging. He leaves me to my own devices as I aim for Gabrielle, high heels sinking into the brilliant green, manicured lawn. My heart accelerates with every step.

Gabrielle says nothing when I come to a stop about twenty feet away from her, frowning, anxious, and perplexed. I watch her, pulse racing, as she brings a finger to her lips and winks at me—slyly, slowly, sensually, her mouth angling up at the corners.

My heartbeat begins to pound for a different reason...

And then Gabrielle points at the leafy branches of the tree she's standing beneath.

My frown deepens as I take a few steps closer, glancing up into the tree, trying to peer through the thick greenery, because I thought I just caught a glimpse of something... Wait. Was that *movement*? There's a rustling overhead, and

I see a fleeting movement again: whatever it was, it looked bigger than a bird, bigger than a squirrel. It was dark, with long arms, and it actually reminded me of a—

I gasp as I stare into the chimpanzee's brown eyes. The animal blinks uncertainly at me, hiding its body a little more behind the trunk of the tree as it grips a branch above its head, maintaining its balance effortlessly.

Without a moment's pause, I turn around and run back over the grass, heels sinking into the ground, to find Scott balancing the camera on his shoulder, all ready for me as he adjusts the lens.

"What's up?" he asks, but I just shake my head, shushing him with a wave of my hand as I glance toward the reporters and cameramen gathered around the park.

"Follow me, okay?" I tell him quietly. He stares at me, one brow raised, but, to his credit, doesn't ask me to explain. Scott has never questioned me in all of the years we've worked together, and, apparently, he's not going to start today. Instead, he follows me as I guide him over the lawn; together, we make a beeline for Gabrielle, still leaning against the trunk of the tree, hands in her pockets, utterly relaxed, as if she doesn't have a care in the world.

I realize, suddenly, that Scott might not be able to see Gabrielle, because he isn't paying any heed to the fact that there's a tall, attractive

111

woman leaning against a tree, wearing a fancy suit and sneakers. Instead, his head is tilted back, and he's staring upward. Though my favorite thing to do, at this point in my life, is to gaze at Gabrielle, I tear my eyes away from my guardian angel's smiling face and look up, too.

And I see the renegade chimpanzee in the tree, far above us.

It's obviously still trying to hide, positioning its gangly body behind the tree trunk and peeking around it. The hiding spot is a pretty good one, all things considered, but there are gaps in the highest branches, and the animal's body is somewhat visible now between the leaves. Scott, after nodding to me, quietly and surreptitiously sets up his shot, trying not to act as if anything interesting is going on so as to avoid alerting the other reporters.

I watch as Gabrielle pushes off from the tree with her hip, and—shoving her hands into her pants pockets as she grins widely at me—she saunters over.

"Thanks for the tip," I whisper to her.

Scott moves away, walking closer to the tree, his eye glued to the viewfinder as he adjusts his zoom.

I regard Gabrielle warmly and tuck a strand of hair behind my ear, smiling at her. I can't help but smile at her.

She bends toward me, her mouth slanting upward as her turquoise eyes gleam. "My pleasure entirely," she whispers, returning my smile and lifting one brow. She leans a little closer: "I do exist to serve you, after all."

I breathe out, staring at the angel for a long moment as my heart knocks against my ribs, blood pounding through my veins in a hot rush. Gabrielle licks her lips slowly, deliberately, and then she reaches up, her long fingers smoothing that same curl of my hair behind my ear again. It's an obnoxious curl that has popped out of the pins I've been using to hold it down with all day, but when Gabrielle touches it, it stays where she puts it, her fingers grazing against my ear.

Everything that I am shivers beneath her touch; I hold Gabrielle's gaze, my heart racing. For a long moment, she says nothing, only cups her hand against my cheek, her body warm against me, her palm hot upon my face. Then she straightens, clearing her throat as she turns away, her hands carefully shoved into her pockets again.

She chews on her lower up, glances up at the tree that Scott is currently filming. "Besides," she tells me with an elegant shrug, "that poor guy up there has an awful tummy ache. He hasn't eaten since last night's banana. He's got to get back home and chow down." She gives me a meaningful glance. "And you can help him get there."

"Yeah. Yeah, we'll do that," I say quietly,

taking my phone out of my purse. Pulse still hammering at an uneven rhythm, I look up the emergency number for the zoo and then dial it as Scott circles the tree carefully, capturing the chimpanzee from all angles. The animal appears more relaxed, staring down at Scott curiously, as if he's amused. Occasionally, the chimp scratches his nose with a twig he picked off of the tree; then he nibbles on the end of the stick thoughtfully, like he's hoping it will turn into something tastier, maybe a piece of fruit.

"Hello, this is the Franklin Park Zoo," says a guy's gruff voice on the end of the line. "Do you have a tip on the chimp?"

"Yes. Um, hi, this is Erin McEvoy with BEAN News," I tell the zookeeper, squaring my shoulders and reminding myself, despite my twitterpated state, that I'm a professional. "And I can see the chimp right from where I'm standing. He's outside of the zoo in a maple tree that's very close to the northeast parking lot."

"Hey, thanks!" the guy tells me. Then it sounds as if he drops the phone, but I can still hear him shouting in the background excitedly, telling his co-workers that the chimp has been spotted.

"Go for it," Gabrielle tells me then, offering an encouraging wink.

"Right. Scott, do you have the live feed?" I murmur, eyeing the rest of the reporters near the front of the zoo. No one seems to have caught on to our scoop yet. So far, so good. Scott nods to me, holding up an *okay* sign with his thumb and forefinger.

I call the station, and Brian answers grumpily. He sounds even more bored and put out when I identify myself.

I ignore his sourness; I'm too excited to let him bring me down. "We have a live feed for the chimp, if you want to patch us in," I tell him.

He makes a surprised snort then, but he agrees to it with a grumble. I nod to Scott, clear my throat, and step in front of the camera.

"This is Erin McEvoy with BEAN, on the scene of a little bit of monkey business," I tell the camera warmly.

Over Scott's shoulder, I glimpse Gabrielle gazing at me with a soft expression, chin raised, turquoise eyes warm and alert.

"This little guy"—I point up toward the tree—"was spotted today enjoying an unplanned vacation," I tell the camera, even as I notice, over Gabrielle's shoulder, the other reporters and camera crews catching on to the fact that we've begun to broadcast live.

"But don't worry," I say with a bright smile. "The chimp went missing last night, and he's probably hungry, but other than that, he looks bright-eyed and uninjured. I just got off the phone with the zookeepers, and they're on their way to fetch him home and treat him to a welcome-back dinner. So, soon this story will have a happy ending for everyone involved."

I sign off, and Scott gives me a high-five as, finally, a team of uniformed zoo staff comes trotting out from one of the doors marked *employees only* in the zoo wall. The other reporters are trying to set up and make quick broadcasts, but the whole ordeal is over in a minute or two as a very patient zookeeper calls out for the chimpanzee, and the chimp, chirping loudly, races down the tree trunk and flings himself into the zookeeper's arms, eliciting *awwws* from everyone watching.

As I turn off my microphone, I glance around, looking for Gabrielle. Amid all of the hubbub with the zookeepers arriving and the reporters scrambling to cover the breaking news story, Gabrielle disappeared.

"Good work," Scott tells me, clapping me on the shoulder as he begins to pack up the equipment.

"Thanks, Scott," I tell him with a distracted smile. I had hoped to have a chance to talk to Gabrielle, to thank her for tracking down the chimp for us, to just...bask in her presence, really, after this, my most triumphant news story. Or what became a triumphant news story because of her.

On the way back to the news station, there's a shadow racing alongside the van, a shadow with feathered wings, and though I still wish I'd been able to speak to her, it comforts me to know that she's right there, that she's with me now.

I gaze at the shadow, my chin cradled in my hand as I think about Gabrielle. Unbidden, my thoughts turn to her expression as she licked her lips, gazing into my eyes with fierce brightness. My thoughts turn to her wanting expression, her lips parting as she reached up and brushed her fingers against my cheek...

"Hey, is it hot in here?" asks Scott, glancing over, startling me out of my reverie. I turn to him, blinking. "I can turn the AC up," he offers, smiling.

"Oh..." I clear my throat, massage the back of my neck as I try to appear breezy, nonchalant. "Sure. I'm kind of warm."

"You're red all over," says Scott, with an easygoing shrug. "So I thought you might be overheated."

"Yeah," I tell him, feeling my flush deepen. "I guess I am, um, overheated."

I pat my too-warm cheeks and try not to think about Gabrielle anymore—or, you know, the anxiety-inducing fact that an angel is guarding me from some impending doom. I try not to think about anything at all, but when I close my eyes, I can still see her eyes, her mouth, her hands...

I nestle down in my seat and sigh as cold air-conditioning blasts over my blushing face.

It's been a long day, and even though I'm tired, I'm also restless. When I leave the station, walking down the concrete steps to the sidewalk bordering the street, I lift my gaze to take in the summer sun still high in the sky. There are hours left in the day, hours full of possibility. But I'm too exhausted to take advantage of any of them. I study my shoes, reflecting that I want to go home, maybe take a relaxing bubble bath...

Then I look up, senses tingling. Because Gabrielle is striding down the sidewalk toward me, a large smile spread across her face. "Hello, Erin," she tells me warmly, tucking a strand of her satiny brown hair behind her ear as she cocks her head toward me.

"Hey," I greet her, smiling, too, and without another word, she takes my arm, twirls me around, and we begin to walk together in the direction *opposite* to my apartment.

"Uh... Where are we going?" I laugh, as she tugs me along companionably.

She chuckles. "I'm sorry to disappoint you, but there aren't going to be any Lifetime movies tonight, Erin," Gabrielle tells me, turquoise eyes twinkling as her smile deepens. "We're going to celebrate your big story!"

I sigh, shake my head. "That's sweet, but it wasn't that big in the grand scheme of —"

"Well, it was immeasurably big for Chompers, I'd say," Gabrielle tells me emphatically.

I stare at her for a long moment before I ask, confused, "Chompers?"

"The chimpanzee, of course!" Gabrielle tells me, grinning.

I laugh a little, and she casts me a sidelong glance. "Let me guess," I begin, raising a brow. "You can speak Chimpanzee, and Chompers told you his name?"

"Precisely." She isn't joking. And I have no choice but to believe her. I mean, if I can believe in guardian angels, I suppose I can believe in an angel who communicates with animals. Not much of a stretch.

"Anyway, c'mon," she tells me, her voice pleading as she, again, tugs on my arm. "Let's do something *different* tonight. Something...oh, I don't know. Something a little...*wild*."

My breath catches in my throat as we pause on the sidewalk and turn toward one another. We're standing very close, a breath away, a kiss away... Gabrielle's face is only inches from my own. She takes my hands and holds them gently, squeezing them so softly, so familiarly that my heartbeat quickens, *races* — just from that one small touch. If she were ever to kiss me, to *really* kiss me, I'm afraid that my heart might explode...

"Something wild?" I whisper. I hold her

119

gaze. "I...I don't know, Gabrielle. You plus the word *wild* makes me nervous..." I trail off, searching her eyes as butterflies whirl in loops in my stomach.

She says nothing for a long moment, only watches me, as if she's trying to figure me out. I take a deep breath, gazing up into her bright turquoise eyes. The same turquoise eyes I've been seeing in my dreams every night since we met, dreams that I've never told Gabrielle about, would be *mortified* to tell her about.

The dreams are becoming increasingly erotic, my subconscious re-envisioning, night after night, that moment when Gabrielle rose over me just after the accident. She arcs above me, and then her mouth claims mine, her body pressed hard against me—

It's gotten to the point that I look forward to the dreams... I experience something in them that I've never experienced with Gabrielle in my waking life.

But there's more to those dreams than the physical aspect. It's the feeling they give me, this...assurance. As if, despite the increasingly chaotic world bustling around us, everything is fine, is more than fine. Everything will always be fine, as long as we're together.

As I hold her gaze now, I think about how much I've come to trust this woman, this angel, though I haven't known her for very long.

"I trust you," I tell her then. Because I've

been thinking it for days, and it's right to tell her now. It's the truth.

"Good," she says softly, and again, she squeezes my hands before threading my arm through the crook in her elbow. We walk down the sidewalk, and I don't know where I'm being taken, but Gabrielle is smiling secretly, warmly, and it's true, what I said: I trust her.

We end up taking the T to the Public Gardens. Sitting beside an angel on the subway may be the most surreal moment of my life thus far—but then again, isn't every moment that I spend with Gabrielle surreal? When we arrive at our destination, the sun is slipping toward the horizon, and the sky is a brilliant blue that takes my breath away. I realize, with a secret smile, that it's the same color as Gabrielle's eyes.

I bought some coffee on my way here, and—honestly? I'm glad we didn't go straight home, no matter how tired I am. There are a lot of things that I'm learning from Gabrielle, but here's one of the biggest lessons: today is all we ever have.

Gabrielle's smile beams as brightly as the sun as we stroll from the T stop into the Public Gardens. We're aiming for the big pond when I realize what Gabrielle has planned.

"Tickets for two, please," she asks the attendant at the swan boats.

The swan boats are a beloved, if kitschy, landmark of the city. They are exactly what they sound like — boats shaped like swans that you can rent and row over the pond. I haven't been in one of the boats in years, but I remember how fun it always was, silly and celebratory at the same time. Ginger and I rented one on the day we both graduated from college. Now that I think about it, I've never shared a boat with anyone aside from Ginger. Melinda was afraid of the water and would have never considered taking a boat ride with me.

The thing about the swan boats is that they're considered to be one of the most romantic things you can do in Boston. They're a staple for all those people wanting to propose, or the thing you naturally choose after a hallmark anniversary dinner. Gabrielle is an angel — surely she had no idea that riding in a swan boat with someone is considered to be romantic. The last time that I rowed with Ginger, we were laughing hysterically the entire time, because every other boat out on the pond that day was occupied with what we immaturely dubbed "kissy couples." We were fresh out of college, but we were also giddy and drunk, which accounts for our juvenile giggling.

Gabrielle, I have to remember, is from a different culture, a different way of life. She probably picked up a brochure for the swan boats and thought they looked like a fun way to spend an evening.

Still...I *wish* — wishing as hard as I can —

that she really did know what sharing a swan boat together means.

God, being so close to her all the time and yet not nearly as close as I long to be... It's driving me *crazy*.

We step off of the rickety dock into the closest white, bird-necked boat. The cloudless sky is reflected perfectly in the still water—until Gabrielle dips her oars beneath the surface. The reflection swirls then, lost, as she begins to row away from the dock.

Even though it's Friday evening and a gorgeous day, there aren't that many other swan boats out on the pond with us. I reach down and dip my fingers into the cool water, taking a deep breath. "God, this is so beautiful," I whisper, staring up at the sky, looking down at the pond shimmering all around us, the divine blue reflecting on its surface... Then I turn my eyes to Gabrielle, sitting across from me in the boat. When I was talking about the scenery being beautiful, a part of me was also talking about her.

"Beautiful, sure. But this isn't exactly...*wild*," Gabrielle admits with a little chuckle, pulling on the oars again. "Still, it's out of the ordinary, isn't it? A break from our usual routine. I thought you'd like that," she says, flashing me a small, brilliant smile. "Granted, it's not a Lifetime movie or a carton of ice cream," she adds thoughtfully, "but I still thought you might enjoy an evening out." Her lips curl up wryly at the corners as she winks.

"Oh, come on, this could totally be part of the plot of a Lifetime movie," I tell her with a little laugh. "Think about it." I hold up a finger when she begins to protest. "A beautiful woman luring me out into a boat on a pond. *Presumably* to kill me and collect the insurance money. That's just one scenario, obviously," I smile. "I've got a million others, because, at this point, I'm fairly certain I've seen every Lifetime movie ever made. I should probably give up reporting and become a Lifetime movie screenwriter."

Gabrielle is chuckling as she leans back, rowing forward again, but her eyes remain locked on mine, and she stops laughing after a moment, gazing at me quizzically. "Beautiful?" she asks then, one brow raised.

I clear my throat and lean back in my seat as I try to think of something funny to say, something to break the tension—but then I realize that I don't *want* to break the tension. I want to be honest. I want Gabrielle to know how I feel. "You're beautiful, Gabrielle," I say softly, offering her a shy smile. "I think that's obvious."

"Is it?" Her wide mouth curves with amusement.

"To me, it is." I hold her gaze, trying to appear calm, confident, even as I tug my red skirt down to cover my knees. I wish I were wearing that blue dress, the one that always makes me feel at the top of my game. It has little pearl buttons down the front and a scalloped neckline that shows off the perfect amount of cleavage, accenting the curve where my neck meets my shoulders. The blue dress makes me feel beautiful and, more importantly, in control.

But I'm not wearing my blue dress. I'm wearing my red suit jacket and skirt, clothes that the station wardrobe staff picked out for me, because I just came from work. And, as things stand, my meager confidence is waning beneath Gabrielle's relaxed, cool-blue gaze. I don't want to look away; I want to match her stare... But my heart is hammering in my chest, and I can feel my cheeks turning red.

"Well, thank you," says Gabrielle, the muscles in her arms flexing beneath her jacket as she rows again. "No one's ever called me beautiful before," she says with a thoughtful expression. "I just took the first body that was assigned to me."

My mind glosses over the fact that an angel has never been called beautiful before and focuses, instead, on the concept of a body being "assigned" to someone. "What do you mean?" I ask her, clearing my throat.

She regards me with a raised brow. "It's simple, really. This body was available, so I accepted it." She jerks her chin toward the sky. "*Up there,* you can find a whole storeroom of physical vessels, all ready to be inhabited. They're specially designed for angels, of course. We don't possess bodies already in use. We don't possess humans," she assures me quickly. "I've seen some of your movies where that took place, and it always seems to end badly, doesn't it? Anyway, that's the demons' domain," she murmurs under her breath.

"Oh. I think I understand, but... Well, what are angels *like*?" I ask her, eyes wide with fascination. She's never opened up to me about her life as an angel before; the body-assignment comment is the first piece of information I've gleaned. "If you didn't have a body before this one...what...*were* you, exactly? Were you just a spirit? Were you always you, always Gabrielle?" I ask her, gesturing to encompass her length.

After a pause, she nods. "Yes," she tells me with a small smile. "I think it might amaze a lot of people to realize that angels are just like you humans. We have all of the things that people have that make them, well..." She trails off. "That make them *people*, like thoughts and feelings and emotions, and genders or lack thereof — just like people do. The difference is, we don't have physical bodies to tie everything together into nice, neat little packages. Though we do *want* bodies," she says, her mouth rounding at the corners. "Some of us, anyway. We watch you go about your lives down here, and it all just looks so wonderful—the cupcakes and the falling in love, the swimming pools and the carousels..." She trails off wistfully, her voice soft.

I swallow, gazing at my hands in my lap. "There's more to being a human than that," I tell her gently. "There's pain. There's loss. There are... There are really hard things that humans have to go through. Because for every human who thinks they fall in love..." I swallow again, shaking my head as I remember my breakup with Melinda. My really *painful* breakup with Melinda. "Well, it's just not always that nice, being human," I finish quietly.

"Granted. I would never belittle anyone's hardship, Erin." She meets my gaze sympathetically. "It isn't always nice being human, yes—but sometimes it is. There are the good things, paired with the bad," she tells me resolutely. "*So* many good things. The *life* that you have inside of you, the will to survive, to do your best, to *thrive*... I really believe you all do your best," she tells me softly, peering up at the sky now. "It's obvious. We watch from up there," she says, pointing, "and what we see *astonishes* us. There's a lot of heartache. There are wars and murders, cruelty beyond understanding," she sighs, lowering her gaze to me now. "But there's so much love, too. So much kindness. Over and over again, people surprise us with the wells of kindness and love that they have inside of them. We find that beautiful," she whispers. "The most beautiful thing, really, in the whole wide world."

My heart is thumping hard in my chest as I hold her eyes. "Love?" I murmur.

Gabrielle's lips round up at the corners, and she sighs. There's a long moment of silence between us, and then she repeats the word, one syllable, but she says it with so much reverence, her voice soft, almost caressing, that I'm held spellbound by her.

She whispers, "*Love.*"

I gaze at her across the the boat. I draw in a deep breath.

Gabrielle is so hopeful, the most hopeful person I have ever met. She is brimming over with this almost *tangible* hope; it exudes from her whenever she speaks, whenever she smiles. She really does have faith in humanity, deep faith—despite the fact that many of my fellow humans don't believe in our worth as a species at all. I mean, I'm a news reporter; I've seen my fair share of crime, of callousness, of—let's be frank—human beings being shitty to one another. Over the years, I've encountered so many stories, in print and on television, involving murders, domestic violence, animal cruelty. Sometimes, I've found myself wondering if humanity is just a great big cosmic mistake. We can be so terrible, so cruel, to others as well as to ourselves.

But when Gabrielle waxes poetic about humankind, when she says, so emphatically, that she believes we're all "doing our best," that the love and kindness humanity possesses makes the angels themselves catch their breath... I can't help it. I feel so at peace; her hope becomes my hope, and the world looks brighter all around me.

I feel hope—good, true hope—coursing through my veins, and inhaled with every breath.

And I'd be the first to admit that I've never been a particularly hopeful person.

I want to tell Gabrielle that I'm so happy that she's here. That I'm so happy that she picked me, or was assigned to me, however it works. I'm so happy that we're together now, right now, no matter how long this lasts. Knowing her has made me a better person, has made my life richer, lovelier...

I want to tell her that I'm falling in love with her.

Because I am, I realize suddenly. I sit across from her in that small boat, the realization settling into my bones: I'm falling head over heels in love with the angel who saved my life. She saved my life, and now she's in my life, an integral part of my life—and I'm fairly certain she doesn't have to be. I've been assigned a guardian angel, but that's just it: she's supposed to *guard* me. She's not obligated to take me out on romantic swan boat outings. She's not obligated to help me achieve my first big news story since I started working at BEAN.

She's not obligated to make every day of my life better and brighter. But she does that, anyway. Because that's just who Gabrielle is. She sees something that needs to be fixed, and she fixes it, just like she fixed Sawyer's leg and hip. Just like she fixed a life that I hadn't even realized was boring and predictable and a little bit broken, because it was my life, and I just figured that was the only way I could live it.

I didn't know how good life could be.

Not until I met Gabrielle.

I want to tell her all of these things, but most of all, I want to tell her that I'm falling in love with her. And I think I'm *going* to tell her... I lick my lips, take a deep breath, find a small pool of courage deep inside of me. Yes...I'm going to say it. I'm just going to blurt it out, before I can talk myself out of it—

But I could never predict what happens next.

Because, sitting placidly in this swan boat on the smooth, still surface of the pond, Gabrielle pauses in her rowing, licks her lips, too, her forehead creased with worry. She looks like she's going to say something to me...

And that's when another boat plows right into us.

The swan boats are very small, and

they're propelled by people-power and two oars. So when this other boat slams straight into the side of our swan, it's surprising, the amount of force that the boat had behind it. I realize, a moment later, that that's because it's being manned by a teenage boy who looks utterly mortified at the fact that he's run into us, but his embarrassment is the last thing that I notice, honestly, because the force is enough to rock us violently...

Enough to send the both of us tumbling into the water.

Even though it was warm out today, the water still shocks my skin with its coolness as I splash headlong into the pond. The water closes in over my head, and I open my eyes: the blue-green of the pond water is a blur around me. With some swift kicks, I thrust myself back to the surface, blowing water out of my nose as I wipe the hair from my eyes and try to make sense of my location.

"Oh, my God, oh, my God," the teenage boy is saying over and over again as he peers over the edge of his boat at the chaos his horseplay created. He's sitting in his boat with a girl who looks to be around his age. Maybe they were on a date together; maybe he was showing off to her, displaying his rowing prowess...without looking where he was going.

Hey, I've done worse to impress a girl, so I can't exactly hold it against him.

Gabrielle surfaces beside me, blowing water out of her mouth like a statue in a fountain. She glances sidelong at me as she treads water; then she casts her glittering turquoise gaze on the hapless boy in the nearby boat.

"Seriously, lady, I'm so sorry," says the boy then, and he actually looks like he might pass out, he's so nervous.

"Accidents happen. Think nothing of it," says Gabrielle, but she's not looking at the boy anymore. "Are you all right?" she asks me, lowering her voice and swimming a little closer to me. We bob together nose to nose as she searches my face, her eyes wide with concern. "Did you swallow water down the wrong pipe?" she asks, patting me gently on the back.

I laugh. "I'm fine," I say, grinning at her. "A nice, refreshing swim was exactly what I needed to cool off," I tell her, with a little wink. "Don't worry." I smile at the kid. "We're okay."

He stares down at me, his eyes growing larger, his grimace growing just a bit deeper. "Wait a second," he groans, "are you that lady from the news? From the BEAN channel?"

My mouth drops open—and then I close it quickly as I swallow a gross gulp of pond water.

Considering how long I've been reporting on the streets of Boston, you'd think I'd have gotten recognized before now...but this is a first for me—and another sign that people *really* don't turn to BEAN for their news.

"Yeah," I tell him, almost sheepishly.

"Oh, my God, I ran into the news lady's boat," moans the boy, sinking down into his seat, cradling his head in his hands.

Gabrielle effortlessly slides up and into our own swan vessel—so effortlessly, in fact, that she looks a bit *in*human doing it. Shouldn't the boat have capsized when she hung off of it and pulled herself up? Then again, she's an angel, so that probably means she has an uncanny ability to make herself weightless.

She turns and smiles down at me, offering me a hand.

I take it, gliding my palm over hers, and then Gabrielle pulls me out of the water as easily as she climbed into the boat herself: without a single sign of strain. I sit down on my seat, take a deep breath and start to wring out my hair.

"Seriously, lady, I'm so sorry," the boy says again, and I smile at him, waving my hand.

"It's okay," I tell him, because it is. This situation is pretty hilarious, albeit cold and wet.

Hey, I almost got run over by a car a few days ago. Um...twice, actually. And that puts a lot of things into perspective for me. Is sitting in a swan boat soaking wet *ideal*? No. But then again, neither is being run over. I'm alive, and that's pretty spectacular, whether I'm wet or not.

That being said, I think I need to pay closer attention to my whereabouts in the future.

I've nearly been done in by two cars and a *boat* now.

After a thousand more apologies, the boy rows his swan away, the tongue-tied teenage girl sitting sullenly, her arms folded over her chest, a deliberate pout making her frown. This run-in probably put a damper on their Friday evening, poor kids.

"Sorry about that," Gabrielle chuckles. "I sensed that they were coming toward us, but I can sort of..." She frowns, searching for the right word. "I can *see* when things aren't going to turn out all right, and I knew this would just be a jolly sort of romp, an *adventure* — so I figured it'd be best not to interfere with fate. Does that make any sense?" Smiling, she leans forward and flicks a damp strand of my hair.

"Sort of." I laugh fondly at her. "That poor boy, though," I tell her, shaking my head. "Did you see his face?"

"Not a bad lesson for the kid. It wouldn't be amiss for him to pay closer attention to where he's going from now on," says Gabrielle, still smiling as she raises an eyebrow. "I think it might actually aid him in the future..." She gets a faraway look as she gazes over my head, her voice trailing off.

I nod hesitantly, because I don't know how being an angel works, after all. I don't know whether Gabrielle allowing the boat to run into us might have actually saved the boy's life in the long run. I finish wringing out my hair.

"Erin," Gabrielle says then, shifting her gaze to me as I begin to shake out the soaked edges of my skirt. Her gaze, I realize, was on my legs before she glanced up and into my eyes. I'm surprised, flustered for a moment—why in the world was she looking at my *legs*?—but I draw in a deep breath.

"Yes?" I ask her, the word squeaking at the end. I haven't forgotten what I was about to say to her before the boat plowed into us. I was actually, just now, trying to work up the courage *again* to try to tell her how I feel about her. Well, I was trying to work up the courage...and failing. The whole capsizing incident threw me for a loop.

But Gabrielle looks so serious, and she's so easygoing, it's not often that she looks serious. She clears her throat, her jaw clenching. Her expression changes and, again, for a moment, she looks as if she's about to say something important. Something meaningful. But whatever it is that she was about to say, she decides, in this moment, against it. The moment comes and goes, and then, like nothing happened at all, Gabrielle is smiling her sunny smile again, indicating the dock over her shoulder. "Do you want to go get a hot dog?" she asks me.

"Oh...sure," I tell her, laughing a little. But my laugh is cut short, because Gabrielle

135

reaches across the space between us, and then...

She places her hand on my thigh.

I'm rendered speechless, and my senses are instantly heightened: my face reddening, my blood rushing through me as my entire body comes alive...

And that's when I realize that my clothes are dry.

Gabrielle removes her hand from my thigh with a slight shrug, turning to pick up the oars. "No sense in being wet on such a lovely summer day, is there?" she tells me with a wink, beginning to row back toward the dock.

"Yeah," I say airily, my voice cracking. I reach up and touch my dry curls. "Right," I manage.

Does she know what she does to me? Does she know that touching someone on the thigh like that is an intimate gesture?

Gabrielle has been around humans before. She's watched a lot of old black-and-white movies, and a lot of Lifetime movies, and I'm sure she's aware that certain gestures carry meaning beyond the obvious. I'm fairly certain that it's a universal thing: placing a hand on someone's thigh is either intended to comfort or seduce.

I realize that she probably needed to reach out and touch me in order to use her angelic powers to dry my clothes, and my thigh was the closest thing to her: easy to place a palm there, easy to remove it quickly.

I realize that it was probably an innocent touch, a practical touch.

But it felt anything but innocent and practical to me.

I glance over at the angel rowing the boat. She's so... I mean, she *does* seem pretty innocent. Well, that's probably not the right word for her. She's fascinated by all of us, by this world and all of its people, us humans. That doesn't necessarily make her innocent, I remind myself, as we reach the docks.

As Gabrielle turns in the boat, I lean against one of the closest trees, feeling—in turns—mortified that I was so instantly turned on when Gabrielle barely grazed my thigh, and utterly despondent that she probably did it for no other reason than to dry my clothes.

Perfectly innocent. Isn't that what an angel is *supposed* to be?

I groan at my own ridiculousness. I mean, *who* falls in love with an angel? Who is that much of a masochistic idiot? Why did I have to fall in love with someone who is the book definition of unavailable, impossible?

She's an angel. I'm a human.

This was bound to be impossible.

"Ready?" Gabrielle murmurs into my ear, startling me. I turn to glance toward her and nod, and then she's standing straight, offering her arm to me with a gallant smile.

The Guardian Angel

We walk arm in arm toward the harbor along the looping concrete pathways through the park, and eventually we find a small hot dog cart. I'm pleasantly surprised to see that they offer tofu dogs. Granted, a lot of carts in the city do these days, which I'm pretty grateful for. I order my tofu dog, and Gabrielle does the same, smiling as she pronounces the words, as if they're some kind of tongue twister.

"What's this?" she asks, glancing down at the ketchup that I'm pour over my bun.

"Ketchup," I tell her. "They have it at All That and a Bag of Chips, but I never use any because it dilutes the flavors. But it's great on hot dogs. Here, just try it—I think you'll like it. And this is mustard," I tell her, patting the tub of mustard with its little spout. "And this is relish." I point to the relish box. "I think you should try all of them," I say, taking her cooked tofu dog from the guy and beginning to pump ketchup onto it.

"I trust you," says Gabrielle, and she's smiling when she says it. I can tell that she means it as sort of a joke. Like someone saying, "I trust you," before you take them to a restaurant they've never tried before or a movie they don't know anything about.

But there's more to her words than that.

I think she meant them. Like, *really* meant them.

I blush, smiling, then pump the mustard

onto her tofu dog. When I'm done, I use the spoon to scoop a big dollop of relish onto it, too. Then I hand the overflowing bun over to her.

"It's not a *real* hot dog," I tell her, with a little grimace. "A lot of people don't like tofu dogs, because they don't taste like real hot dogs, so I don't know if you'll like it or not. Fair warning."

"Well, I've never had either. This is another culinary first for me," says Gabrielle, with a big smile. She regards the bun in her hand thoughtfully. "I've seen these in your movies. In quite a few of your movies. They always looked a little funny...and a little tasty," she muses, turning the bun this way and that in her hands. Then she lifts the hot dog up to her mouth and takes a big bite. I do the same.

"Oh," she murmurs around a mouthful. Her turquoise eyes are big and round, and she moans euphorically as she takes another big bite before swallowing that first one. Her mouth is stuffed now, and I'm laughing, because she reminds me of the chipmunks that we have near our office, always filling their little cheek pouches with sunflower seeds that Scott tosses out the door for them.

"This is *so good*," Gabrielle sighs, after chewing and swallowing.

I laugh again, taking another bite.

We begin to walk down the sidewalk, still heading toward the harbor and the piers. The sun is starting to set behind us, over the city, tinging the sky above the ocean with a brilliant, breathtaking fuchsia. The fluffy clouds pillowed around the horizon throw back the colors like a sumptuous painting.

We finish the hot dogs, wiping our hands on napkins before throwing them away, along with the little paper baskets. We finally reach one of the piers and stand shoulder to shoulder companionably, looking out over the bay, at the waves moving across the ocean, at the colors and clouds and the boats peppering the horizon. As I shift my weight, leaning against one of the wooden struts blocking the pier off, our hands gently bump together, the back of my hand brushing against Gabrielle's warm palm. I'm about to say "sorry" and move away, just like I'd do if I bumped up against one of my co-workers, but something stills my tongue.

Gabrielle takes my hand into hers, weaving her fingers through mine, her palm warm and comfortable.

My heartbeat thunders through me. It's pounding so loudly that I'm afraid Gabrielle will be able to hear it: angels probably have super-hearing, after all.

I try to talk myself down. She's just holding my hand because that's what she does. She probably saw it on an old movie and thought it was a cute thing that humans do. It's probably nothing more than a friendly gesture.

But, God, I wish it were something more.

I need to tell her. I need to work up the courage and tell her *soon* how I feel, because she needs to know. I need to be honest with her, with this angel sent to guard me. She deserves that much from me.

I didn't mean to start falling in love with you, I think at her, my pulse throbbing in my ears. *But I am. And I don't know what to do about it.*

Overhead, the colors from the sunset paint the sky, the sea reflecting the magenta and fuchsia and violet so magnificently that I stare, mesmerized by the colors, by the salt waves, by the clouds banked along the horizon. Together, we watch the sunset in quiet companionship, our hands entwined.

As the first star peeks out from the heavens, I draw in a deep breath, clearing my throat. "Gabrielle?" I begin quietly.

"Yeah," she murmurs, her gaze still pinned to the spectacular view.

"You thought you saved my life when you pushed me out of the way of those cars, right?" I murmur, glancing at her as I clear my throat.

Gabrielle chuckles a little, shaking her head. "Bit presumptuous of me, wasn't it?"

"No, I mean..." I sigh, turning to face the angel. I hold onto her hand tightly now. "Are you here because..." I can feel my heartbeat accelerate as I ask the question that has lingered, unspoken, between us since Gabrielle first revealed herself to me: "Are you here because I'm supposed to die soon?"

Gabrielle holds my stare for a long moment. Then she bows her head and closes her eyes. When she looks back up at me, her gaze is so bright, so blue. "Not if I have anything to do about it," she tells me, jaw tightening. "And—luckily—I do." She squeezes my hand now, reaching out to take my other one, threading her fingers through my fingers. "See, fate's a tricky thing," she breathes, gazing down at our two hands entwined. "Everything, all of the milliseconds of time, are planned out." Gabrielle lifts her gaze and glances out toward the street, at a bus driving rounding the corner. "Just like a bus schedule. On this date, you'll do this. At this time, you'll do this. But fate, like a bus schedule, isn't set in stone. Sometimes there's snow, or an unexpected flock of geese crossing the road, and the schedule gets delayed or changed altogether. I'm here to change your schedule, Erin."

I smile weakly. "So you're my goose."

"I'm your goose."

I swallow, taking all of this in, and all I can think to say is, "Thank you for being here for me." I whisper those words, but there's so much weight to them. There's so much behind that simple statement.

Gabrielle says softly, "There's nowhere

else I'd rather be." And I know that she means this with all of her heart.

Do angels...*have* hearts?

I find myself looking up at her now, and it's all too much: we're standing too close, she's holding my hands with just enough warmth, too *much* warmth, and I feel overwhelmed by her nearness, her tender expression as she gazes down at me. I gulp down air, but I'm finding it hard to breathe.

The need to do something—*now*—rises in me faster than my common sense can react. I stand a little taller, a little straighter, rising onto my tiptoes, tugging her forward, just a little...

And then I'm kissing Gabrielle.

I'm kissing an angel.

Warmth. Soft warmth. She just ate a tofu dog, and she should probably taste exactly like that, with ketchup and mustard and relish, but she doesn't. Instead, she tastes impossibly sweet, like the most crave-worthy piece of chocolate or candy or cake. Imagine that piece of candy that you always thought about when you were a kid; you couldn't wait until you could get your hands on another piece again. For me, it was those red gummy fish. God, I thought about nothing else until I got another package of them from the little corner store up the road from where I lived. That's what this kiss is like. Crave-worthy and delicious and beautiful and sweet. All of these things, but with heat added to the mix, heat that rushes through me, through us, as I kiss her deeply, unashamed.

My heart rises into my throat as I realize, suddenly, that she's kissing me back.

She *is*.

My guardian angel is kissing me.

She's leaning down, and she's hesitant, in the beginning, as if she's learning, figuring things out, but then she's kissing me with more fervor, fiercer, harder. She's taking my breath away with the strength of the kiss, with the passion that seems to flow through the both of us now, passion bright and unyielding.

Finally, too soon, the kiss ends. We back away, the two of us, and we stare at one another. I'm so afraid, in that moment, afraid of... Well, she could react in a million different ways. What's going to happen now? What if angels aren't supposed to kiss? What if they're not gay—or straight, or anything? What if they can't experience romance or don't find physical affection appealing or...

My rampant questions and abstract fears are suddenly silenced when Gabrielle lets go of my right hand, reaching up. Gently, gently, she cups my neck and the back of my head, and then she's leaning down to kiss me again.

If I thought that first kiss was brilliant, fearless and beautiful...then I had no idea what a kiss with an angel could *really* be like.

Because there's fire behind this kiss now, fire that burns through me in a delicious, consuming way. I am consumed by this kiss, by her mouth on mine, by the way her body presses against my own, by the delicate, gentle way she curves her fingers over the arch of my neck, drawing me closer to her, ever closer, like a star pulls planets near. She kisses me, and in that simple kiss, there is connection beyond description. I love kissing—it's a beautiful, sexy thing to do. It makes you feel closer to your partner as you share yourself, as you make yourself vulnerable to another human being...

But I never thought it could be so intimate, as revealing as sex itself.

And that's what this kiss is. I feel so close to her that we seem to merge together, the angel and me.

This kiss, too, has to end, and it does, the two of us holding one another at arm's length, breathing hard. Gabrielle's turquoise eyes are darkened with exquisite desire, the sort of desire that makes my belly turn to liquid fire, that makes me immediately wet. God, to be gazed at like that...it's all I've ever wanted in my whole life, and I never had the words to wish for it, I realize.

She wants me, utterly.

And, God, I want her.

But then Gabrielle shakes her head a little, clearing her throat, licking her shining lips. She takes a deep breath in and a deep breath out, before she says, "Wow."

And then: "I wasn't supposed to do that."

My heartbeat is thundering through me again, but this time, it's with panic. "You...weren't?" I whisper.

"No, it's...well, forbidden." I stare at her with wide eyes as she shakes her head again, her brow creased. "There's something in the Seraphic rulebook, uh, about fraternizing with mortals. *Don't get personally involved.* Hmm." She gazes at me for a long moment, her brow smoothing, her eyes growing wider, gentler. Then she smiles, her mouth turning up at the corners a little slyly. "Let me just..." she murmurs, and then she leans toward me, bowing her beautiful head, and she kisses me again, deeply, fire burning through me instantly at her touch, as her mouth moves over mine, the sweet taste of her consuming me.

"Problem is," Gabrielle whispers against my lips, "I rather like getting personally involved with you."

I stare up at her, gasping, my blood moving as fast as light through my veins. "That *is* a problem," I whisper back.

"Yeah. It is."

And then we kiss again.

Chapter 5: Declarations

I've never been more tired in my life.

People use that phrase often, but this time, I think it's true. I stare at my bedside clock as it beeps cheerfully — and very, very loudly — at me, informing me that it's six o'clock in the morning. On a *Saturday.* There's something blasphemous about being awake this early on a Saturday, the one day per week that I'm almost guaranteed to have off.

Most Sundays I have to work, but Saturday? That's the day I get to sleep in for as long as Sawyer will permit me — until, finally, she slips her cold, wet nose under the sheets and starts to lick my toes with the adept desperation of a dog who really, *really* needs to have her morning pee, and her mother's longing for a nice, long rest is really her least concern. That's the day that I get to relax, puttering around the house in my bathrobe and worrying about nothing more than what's for dinner. The one day I almost never leave the house, except to walk Sawyer and maybe stock up on ice cream.

But, even though it's Saturday, I stick my feet out from under the blankets now, plunking them heavily on the floor as I yawn, miserably stretching, trying to rub the sleep from my heavy-lidded eyes.

Sure, it's six o'clock in the morning on a Saturday, but Ginger made me promise—*pinky* promise, the most serious kind of promise that we make to one another—that I would drag myself from my indulgent slumber to meet her for the Red Sox home game today.

To Ginger, the Red Sox are a religion. And I made her a promise. I repeat that phrase to myself over and over—*I promised, I promised*—as I hit the alarm button on my clock and blink blearily at the offensive digital numbers glowing back at me.

Granted, waking up at six o'clock in the morning isn't normally a problem for me. When I'm assigned the early morning news, I've got to be air-ready by four a.m., bright-eyed and bushy-tailed—after guzzling down an unhealthy amount of coffee, of course.

So, the problem isn't, truthfully, the early hour—or even the fact that it's a sacred Saturday morning. The problem is that I scarcely slept at all last night. I tossed and turned so much that I became hopelessly tangled in the sheets, and my hair is sticking straight up, Bride of Frankenstein couture.

I couldn't sleep because I was thinking about Gabrielle.

And the kiss. Well, the kiss*es*.

I sigh and try to run my fingers through my hair, but it's too knotted, so I just close my eyes and sigh again. My cheeks warm as I think about last night, being in the swan boat with Gabrielle, kissing Gabrielle... I remember her hands on my hips as I slid my own hands around her curves, my fingers moving slowly to the small of her back, daring to inch just a *tiny* bit beneath her jacket and shirt to caress the soft, hot skin there. How smooth she felt, how sweet she tasted, her turquoise gaze intense, aflame when she broke away from me... Her voice was a low, controlled growl as she spoke my name, repeated it again and again, like a prayer.

My heart thumps hard in my chest as I remember all of that, as I re-experience the thrill, the wonder, the connection... After we came home to my apartment last night, I hoped that things might progress from a few hesitant, unexpected kisses to something more, something deeper.

But...our kisses didn't progress, not even a little bit. They just...stopped. It was jarring, maddening how, despite the desire crackling between us, Gabrielle and I simply backed away from one other, breathing hard and staring into one another's eyes as if to ask, "What now?" A question that neither of us chose to ask out loud, or answer.

Lost in our own private thoughts, we took the T to my exit, walked quietly back to my apartment, and — that was it.

When Gabrielle escorted me to my bedroom, she — again — planted a chaste kiss against the corner of my mouth, the mouth that she'd passionately kissed a mere hour before. Had it only been that long ago? I felt so changed. I felt as if *everything* had changed. But we acted as if nothing had changed at all.

So that's all she did, brushing her lips against my skin, feather-soft, as she bowed her head to me. She whispered, "Good night, Erin," and left me, probably went to the living room, where she sat down on the couch, cracked open that angel book and waited, sleepless, for the morning to come. I stood alone in my bedroom doorway, reaching up to brush my fingers over my lips. I felt stunned, overstimulated. And *really* confused.

Of course, after that, my mind was second-guessing all that had happened between us as I tried to make sense of the mixed signals that Gabrielle has been giving me. She said she wasn't supposed to kiss me. Is that why she stopped? Is that why our romantic evening together ended so abruptly? I considered every word, every gesture, every caress all night long, looping over and over the fact that, after I kissed her, she kissed me back. And then she acted as if it had never actually happened at all.

This whole situation is crazy. Here I am, pondering whether or not my *guardian angel* is attracted to me. Thinking about how my *guardian angel* felt in my arms, how her mouth tasted, how her body felt against mine...

I've had my fair share of experience with crazy. Consider my job. But my life now...it's a whole new level of, "*Seriously?!*"

The crux of the matter is that I've had feelings for Gabrielle from the first moment I saw her, from the first moment I looked into her soul-splitting, piercing blue eyes. And I have asked myself whether I started having feelings for her because she *did,* after all, save my life. I've wondered if this is all based upon something outside of herself, circumstances beyond our control, circumstances that, however temporarily, shoved us together. It's a rotten thought, but adrenaline is a powerful thing. Were my feelings for Gabrielle inspired by what she had done for me, rather than who she is? Have I developed some sort of savior infatuation? It wouldn't be the first time something like that had happened. I've read countless news stories in which a kidnapped woman fell in love with her rescuer, or a crime victim fell for the attorney who brought the case to justice.

And though I wondered about that possibility off and on last night, devoting several hours of tossing and turning to the subject, I know—and I think I always knew—that that my attraction to Gabrielle has nothing to do with her guardianship of me. I've searched my heart backwards and forwards, and I can't deny the truth: There's something about Gabrielle—wings and angelhood notwithstanding—that draws me in, like a moth to a flame. I would be crushing on her, *hard,* whether she were a ballerina or a bodybuilder, an author or a farmer. I just *really* like her. And if I'm beginning to fall in love with her, it's for *her,* for everything that makes her the warm, sparkling, dynamic being that she is.

Unfortunately, that also makes all of this much, much more confusing.

Why did Gabrielle kiss me back if she doesn't feel the same way? I thought about that a lot last night, too, and here's what I came up with: Because she realizes that we can't possibly be together, that—for whatever reason—humans and angels aren't supposed to fall in love, and that after her mission she has to go back home.

She knows that, if we take things further, we'll only end up hurting more in the end.

Now I tilt my head back and stare at the ceiling for a long moment, releasing the longest, heaviest sigh of my life. And then I stand up, wondering where Sawyer could be; then I remember that, since Gabrielle "moved into" my apartment, I have become much less awesome in Sawyer's eyes. She spends most of her time adoring the angel, staring up at Gabrielle with her big brown collie eyes, blinking long lashes—almost flirtatiously. It makes sense. Gabrielle loves Sawyer back; that much is obvious. She always offers my dog an affectionate smile, always scratches her behind the ears in the exact spot that makes Sawyer thump her back leg ecstatically against the floor.

I walk down the hallway, blinking at the bright overhead light, yawning and stretching. And, unsurprisingly, Sawyer is there in my living room, lying in her usual spot on the couch, her sweet, long snout propped up on crossed paws as if she's a dog model posing for a painter. When she sees me, she thumps her tail against the couch cushions, but that's the only part of her that moves. I can tell that Gabrielle already took her out for her morning walk, because Sawyer's leash is looped in a perfect spiral on the coffee table on top of the angel book.

And on my dining room table sits is a steaming bowl of oatmeal, sprinkled with chopped-up peaches, strawberries and...hmm. I walk up to the table and peer closely at the small green splotches in the bowl. It looks as if Gabrielle spooned some relish onto my oatmeal. Well, she's still learning about flavor combinations, what humans like and don't like, and she was awfully keen on the relish on her hot dog last night...

Who knows? Maybe relish will taste *amazing* on oatmeal.

I put my hands on my hips and bite my

153

lower lip.

Gabrielle, herself, is nowhere to be seen.

I know she must be nearby. She told me that she has to stay around me all of the time, "just in case" something unexpected happens, though occasionally, for practical purposes, she chooses to make herself invisible.

But why wouldn't she be visible now?

Anxiety twists my stomach as I pull out my chair and sit down on it, drawing the bowl of oatmeal toward me with a sigh.

Does she regret last night? Does she regret kissing a human...or just kissing me?

Does she regret getting assigned to be my guardian angel?

Slow down, Erin. It isn't like me to jump to the worst possible conclusions, but I'm exhausted and overemotional—because I *did* nearly die recently, and I *do* have a guardian angel, which is abnormal by any stretch of the imagination, bound to make you rethink, oh, I don't know, your entire *worldview*. And, damn it, I know I'm falling for Gabrielle. There's something that tugs me toward her, as if our hearts are connected by strings...

And now she's here, but she's invisible, *hiding* from me—because she doesn't want to talk to me?

To put it bluntly, that really hurts.

Despite the oddness of peaches, strawberries, and relish mixed with oatmeal, I am determined to choke down the entire sweet/sour bowl, because Gabrielle made breakfast for me, and it was a sweet gesture, whether she's choosing to be visible now or not. I just...wish she would materialize; I wish I could talk to her about last night. I wish I could tell her all of the things that I want to tell her. I wish she would talk to me about her own feelings, her own wants and worries.

I lift a spoonful of oatmeal to my mouth thoughtfully. I guess I could call out to her, ask her to appear... I swallow, suddenly nervous. And then what would I do, exactly?

I mulled over our *kiss* predicament all night long, but I still have no idea what she's going to say when I bring the topic up. And that really scares me. Because, of course, she could tell me that the kiss was a mistake. That she shouldn't have done it, that she regrets it, that she needs me to know that we can never do anything like that again. Though it's contrary to her personality, I can imagine her saying these things, her voice and face stern—and the mere imagining makes my heart ache with loss...

If that's what Gabrielle is going to tell me, I don't want to hear it. I don't want to know. Not yet. I want last night to remain perfect in my memory, unburdened, as if it just happened a heartbeat ago.

I don't want to let go of last night, of Gabrielle. I'm not ready to lose my chance with her.

As I stand up, holding the empty oatmeal bowl in my right hand, I inhale sharply, gripping the edge of the table with my left hand. The bowl *thumps* back down to the table as I breathe in,, slowly this time, closing my eyes. Because there was a scent in the air...a scent that I hadn't realized I associated so strongly with Gabrielle. But, I realize suddenly, this scent...this is what Gabrielle smells like.

It has an overtone of jasmine. Soft, white flowers, star-shaped, delicate and ethereal, yet strong. And there's something warm beneath the floral note, like a sweet, earthy vanilla, and a little caramel.

It's such an intoxicating, beautiful perfume, not at all overbearing. There's just a trace of it surrounding me, flitting by me, as if my invisible guardian angel just walked past my shoulder...

As if she crossed in front of me and — for a secret, stolen heartbeat — lingered.

I draw in a deep breath, trying to hold onto the scent for a moment longer, but it has already dissipated. Gabrielle has already moved away from me, drifting invisibly, silently, like a ghost.

For a long moment, I wrestle with myself. I open my mouth; I'm going to speak her name, and then she's going to appear. And then, face to face, the two of us will sit down and talk about last night, about what last night meant to the both of us—even if it meant vastly different things.

But anxiety seizes me. I'm just not ready. I can't do this. I close my mouth, sighing heavily through my nose.

I walk back down the hallway toward my bedroom, shut my door and lean against it, closing my eyes, resting a hand on my stomach. I take a few deep breaths as emotion wells up into my throat, filling my eyes with tears as I try to imagine a world in which an angel and a human can be in a romantic relationship together...

And I can't imagine it at all.

Sure, I've seen movies where humans fell in love with angels—and their romances always turned out happily in the end. But life isn't a movie. And Gabrielle and I are two different creatures from two immeasurably different worlds. I know better than to wish for something that's impossible.

But if that's true...why am I wishing for it *so hard*, anyway?

Miserable and frustrated, I dress in the Red Sox jersey that Ginger gave me as a gift last Christmas. I'm not much of a fan of sports, including baseball, but Ginger insisted that I have a jersey to wear for all the games we go to together. I'm starting to learn a lot about baseball, honestly, from simple immersion.

The Guardian Angel

Besides, Ginger loves the Sox so much that I feel as if I have a best-friend duty to support her in her interest/obsession. I pull my hair up into a ponytail after brushing it hard—which results in my normally curly hair amassing itself into one giant blonde pouf.

I put on my makeup, slide my legs into some skinny jeans, and, feeling exhausted and not really up to this excursion at all—I just want to climb back into bed and wallow in my uncertainties—I remind myself how much I love my best friend...

And then I'm outside.

Ginger is just pulling up to the curb in front of my apartment building as I close the front door behind me. Even though I'm trotting down the concrete steps toward her, she's already honking the horn of her Jeep, practically laying on top of it.

"We're already late!" she calls out to me, as I hurry up to the car, fling open the passenger side door and slide into the seat. She guns the engine, and we pull away from the curb into traffic so quickly that I think we're going to rear-end the taxi in front of us...until Ginger slams on the brakes, neatly and calmly—nearly hurling me out the front window. But, hey, at least we didn't hit the car. I sheepishly pull the seat belt over my shoulder as she swears at the taxi driver.

Then she gives me a huge smile. "Hi,

sweetie, how are you?" Ginger may have just turned the air blue around us with obscenities, but those expletives aren't a real indication of Ginger's actual mood.

She's going to Fenway Park, the home of her beloved Red Sox.

So Ginger is one-hundred-percent *ecstatic.*

"Oh, my God, this is so *awesome,* seriously, Erin. I'm just so, so glad you could come today," she chirps chirruping beside me as she switches lanes like a crazy person, almost causing the big SUV behind us to smash into our bumper. Luckily, at the last possible second, the driver is able to brake and swerve a little, though he points a rude gesture toward us through his open window.

Ginger, unconcerned, goes on cheerfully: "I've been so excited about this game. I mean, come on, they're playing against the Yankees, and they just *barely* got that win against them last time. You know the Yanks are going to be after revenge, so the Sox had better be on their A game."

I smile at Ginger, who's beaming as she stares at the road. "I know how excited you were about this game," I tell her. "I honestly wouldn't miss this for the world."

"Thanks, but... Hey, are you okay?" she asks me then, glancing over, her brow furrowed with worry. "I mean, I know baseball isn't your favorite thing, but you're not usually as...well, subdued as this. What's up?"

"Oh..." I trail off, peering out the window with a shake of my head, my cheeks automatically (and mutinously) blushing crimson. "It's nothing," I tell her.

Ginger tosses me the catcher's mitt that was resting on her lap as she makes a turn so hard, the car is practically on two wheels; rubber screeches beneath us. "I have something that'll cheer you up," she tells me then, her lips turning up at the corners mischievously.

I raise a single brow, because Ginger's tone is cloying, wheedling, which can only mean she's going to talk about—

"Rachel's single again," Ginger announces triumphantly, just as I suspected she would. She always uses this tone of voice when she's in the mood to set me up.

I sigh and lean against the back of the seat, shaking my head in chagrin as I chuckle mirthlessly. "Ginger—"

"Hey, take this seriously," she admonishes me, though she can't stop herself from grinning. "Rachel and her girlfriend broke up two nights ago, and when I talked to Rach yesterday at work, she told me that it was 'for good this time.' And, I mean, I know she said that last time, too, but she looked as serious as *death* about it, when I asked her. So...I was thinking...if you want to give a date with Rachel another go..."

I shake my head, blushing more deeply as I gaze out the window. I clear my throat, gathering my thoughts. "I thought they were very much in love... Rachel and her girlfriend."

Ginger shrugs. "Who knows? All *I* know is that Rachel is available right now. And I've gotten to know Rachel pretty well. She's kind of perfect for you, so—"

"I just don't think..." But I can't finish my sentence. I bite my lip, my cheeks so hot now that I'm beginning to feel a little feverish.

And, even though the traffic is starting to thicken as we aim for Fenway Park, Ginger turns her attention from the packed street that she *should* be watching and points her stare toward me, instead, her eyes growing wide at first, and then narrowing in suspicion.

"Wait a *second*," she says, swearing under her breath again as she almost rear-ends a moving van in front of us; with lightning-fast reflexes, she swerves into another lane. I grip the handle of my door and manage not to sway too much in my seat. "Why don't you want to date Rachel, Erin? I mean, really?" she asks me then, waggling her eyebrows and drawing out the words. After a moment, a huge smile breaks over her face. "Huh? Why *don't* you? You know I know you, sweetheart. I can read you like a *book*—"

I sigh.

"And by your blushing and acting all

moody, my only deduction, dear Watson, is that you must be seeing someone!"

"Come on. Can't a girl blush and feel moody once in a while?" I murmur back, as I glance into the backseat, wondering if Gabrielle is in the car with us. I don't see her shadow beside us on the pavement, and since she has to stick around me, wouldn't that mean she's very close, within listening distance? God, I can't talk about this now. Especially not if she's here, listening.

"Truth?" prompts Ginger, one brow raised.

"Okay, okay," I mutter, straightening from my slump in the seat. I take a deep breath. Once Ginger is on to something, she's a little like a bloodhound: there is not a world in which she's going to let a subject go—not until she finds out everything she wants to know about it.

I sigh and roll my eyes with a groan. "So, I'm not actually *seeing* anyone," I tell her, then, which is totally the truth. Well. Not *totally* the truth. And I don't lie to Ginger. I clear my throat. "I mean..." I think about how I can possibly phrase this. "I'm not seeing anyone *exactly—*"

"Spill, Erin," Ginger commands.

"It's...complicated," I tell her with a little grimace. God, it's *so* complicated, I don't even know where to begin. And I love Ginger, and I trust her with my life...but I really don't think I can tell my best friend that I'm falling in love with an angel.

Ginger is pretty open-minded, but I think this one is a stretch of giant proportions. For one, she wouldn't believe me—how could she? She'd think I was joking, stalling... And then, if I pressed on doggedly, clinging to my story, she'd begin to wonder about my sanity. You know, just like *I* wondered about my sanity when I was seeing winged shadows following me everywhere.

No one in their right mind would ever believe that I have a living, breathing guardian angel.

So how could anyone ever believe—or empathize with the fact—that I have feelings for this impossible, mythical angel?

"Oh, it's always complicated," Ginger teases, rolling her eyes as she tosses a grin at me. She veers toward the parking ramp of one of the garages surrounding the baseball stadium. "Just open up a little," she begs. "Give me a bone. What's her name?"

At that moment, I feel a warm breath against my neck, and every inch of my body shivers in response to it.

Gabrielle *is* here. She's in the car with us, in the backseat. All at once, I notice her perfume: the faint, warm scent of jasmine flowers.

She's here, and she's listening.

My blush deepens, and my heart begins to beat triple-time in my chest.

I draw in a deep breath, and then I just...*say* it. "Her name is Gabrielle," I whisper, lingering on the syllables of her name as I exhale them. It's such a beautiful word, I realize. Almost as beautiful as she is.

I feel another warm breath on my neck, and I hear a sound like a sigh next to my ear. A happy sigh? I can't tell. I swallow and bite my lower lip.

"So...what's she like?" asks Ginger, taking a payment ticket from the little machine at the parking garage entrance.

At that moment, I can feel feather-light fingertips grazing the back of my neck, trailing a long, soft line from the edge of my ponytail all the way down to where my shoulders are visible in the Red Sox jersey. I shiver again—I can't help it. That one, tiny sensation has me melting into a puddle of goo.

But what does it mean, that caress?

I'm way overthinking this...as usual.

"She's..." And then I'm grinning in spite of myself. "She's divine," I tell Ginger, and I chuckle quietly, because what I just said is ridiculous *and* accurate.

"Oh, my God," Ginger murmurs then, glancing at me with wide eyes as she rolls into an empty space, throwing her car into park and turning off the engine. She stares at me for a long moment, her eyes narrowed as she jingles the keys in her hand. Then she says in a very low voice, "Erin. You're in *love* with her!"

"What?" I blink; my throat is suddenly dry. I start to protest. No, I'm not *in* love with her. Not...quite. I keep wondering if all of these feelings warring inside of me really do indicate that I've fallen in love with Gabrielle, but when I continue to protest Ginger's accusation, the words feel wrong, untrue. *Am* I in love with Gabrielle? Like, seriously and absolutely? The kind of falling-in-love that's real and lasting, not just warm, sappy feelings and mushy thoughts. Is this real and true *love?* I know I was feeling it last evening, but then I spent a long, sleepless night tossing and turning and second-guessing *everything*, and I guess I talked myself out of the fact that I was heart-linked to m angel...

But what does it mean if I am, if I'm really in love with Gabrielle? She said herself that it was forbidden...that *this* is forbidden. Us. Gabrielle has a job to perform with me. All she has to do is keep me safe, and after the terrible thing that's scheduled to happen to me finally happens (or almost happens, since Gabrielle is here to save my life, to keep me alive and kicking), she'll return to heaven, or Seraphim HQ, or wherever it is that Gabrielle lives when she's not guarding a hapless mortal.

Gabrielle will leave. You're not allowed to keep your guardian angel forever. That isn't how the system works. Gabrielle made that perfectly clear.

And then? She'll be gone. And all of this, everything between us, will be over. Poof. Vanishing like smoke in the wind.

I hadn't allowed myself to consider what would happen if we started a relationship together, Gabrielle and me. I hadn't mulled over the thought, and I certainly hadn't considered what would happen afterward, when Gabrielle leaves. But now, right *now*, the inevitability of our parting weighs heavily upon me as I sit in Ginger's Jeep, feeling the void Gabrielle will leave behind, possibly very soon, pressing down on my shoulders. On my heart.

I've gotten so used to having Gabrielle around—there for breakfast, there when I get home from work, there for lunch... I've gotten so used to spending my hours with her that the thought of her absence makes my heart hurt.

Now that I've been living with Gabrielle, I realize we've been co-habitating as if it is the easiest, most natural thing in the world. And I can't imagine going through the minutiae of my day-to-day life—eating ice cream, watching crappy movies, going on small, spontaneous adventures—without Gabrielle by my side.

Or, you know, as the case may be, floating slightly above me.

I am *in love with her,* I admit to myself, really and truly.

Apparently, my silence is confirmation enough for Ginger. She's smiling as she glances sidelong at me, pocketing her keys, but her smile is fleeting. "So if you're in love," she says slowly, carefully, watching me closely, "then why do you look so sad?"

I take a deep breath.

I realize, with a pang of guilt, that I can't express my inner turmoil to my best friend. I can't tell her that the *divine* object of my affection is an *angel*. I just can't. I can't tell her that this is the reason for my sadness: knowing it's impossible for us to be in a relationship, that there can never be an "us" at all.

I want there to be an "us." I want it more than I've wanted anything in a very, very long time. Maybe more than I've ever wanted anything.

I gulp down another deep breath, tears coming to my eyes, and I look skyward for a moment, trying to make certain those stupid tears stay put. I don't want Ginger to see how upset I really am, and more than that, I don't want Gabrielle to know how much all of this is hurting me.

"Hey, is your hat new?" I venture weakly, glancing at Ginger's ensemble.

Ginger is probably the biggest Red Sox fan in the world, and she often boasts that she possesses a sample of every Red Sox cap ever made, including one that an original player wore in whatever decade it was that the Red Sox got together. She won the hat at a Sotheby's auction for a small fortune. The hat she's wearing now looks brand-new, and it actually looks handmade—in a good way—with a pair of felt socks hand-stitched neatly onto the baseball cap's brim.

"Yes, it is," says Ginger, preening a little before she snorts. "Hey, nice change of the subject, by the way." She scoops her catcher's mitt off of my lap and puts it on her hand, pummeling the center of her now leather-clad palm. "Just...whatever's going on with you," Ginger begins, sighing as she glances out the front window of the car at the concrete wall beside us, "know that you deserve to be happy, okay?"

I stare at her, my brow furrowed.

"I'm serious." She sighs again, this time in exasperation. And then my best friend leans over and hugs me tightly. "I'm so tired of seeing you hook up with the wrong women. There's someone out there for you. I can feel it in my gut." She pats her stomach with her catcher's mitt as she leans away from me. "Okay?" she says, staring me fiercely in the eyes.

I want to tell her the truth so badly right now it hurts. But I don't want to ruin the day for her. I don't want to put Ginger in a position where she'll have to wonder about her best friend's mental state. And I could never fault her for that. Could *anyone* believe their friend if they told them that they were falling for a real-life angel, wings and all? Would I believe *her* if she told me the same? No. I'd be worried about her, very worried...

"So, let's go!" says Ginger, brightening a little. "Who knows? Maybe today's the day I catch that mythical foul ball!"

"Ginger," I chuckle, unbuckling my seat belt, "you say that *every* game."

"Hey, you never know," she tells me with a wink as we get out of the car.

Ginger already bought our tickets, so we skirt around the lines at the ticket counters. As we aim for our seats, I think about Gabrielle's presence in the car. Ever since her invisible fingers caressed the back of my neck, and I felt her breath against me, smelled her scent, I haven't sensed her around me at all. But I know she's nearby. And the knowledge comforts me, despite my anguished heart.

Even if I don't know what's going to happen between us, I have to keep remembering that right here, right now, I'm not faced with any big questions or decisions. Right here and now, it's just a beautiful Saturday morning, and I'm spending it with my best friend at Fenway Park. And that's worth celebrating.

An important lesson that my almost-dying taught me. This moment is really the only one that matters. That's what I try to tell myself, at least, whenever I stray from *this moment* and begin to worry about the future. And, for the most part, it's working. Before my near-misses, I tended to worry about the future quite a bit more than I do now—angsting about my love life (or lack thereof), my career, and just about everything else.

And these moments, basking in the bright sunlight of Fenway Park as Ginger and I lean back in our seats, are pretty awesome. Or they are until I realize that I have to use the bathroom.

Of *course* I have to use the bathroom: I've consumed two large Cokes in about twenty minutes. It's hot out today, and my jersey is kind of heavy. And, to tell the truth, *I love Coke*, even though I know the high fructose corn syrup is bad for me.

"I'll be right back," I tell Ginger, who nods at me, though she really isn't paying any attention to what I just said. She mutters something about the bases being loaded. With my limited knowledge of the rules of baseball, I suspect that based loaded is a pretty good thing for the Red Sox, who are up to bat.

"I'll only be a second," I promise Ginger, who waves a hand at me, never peeling her eyes off of the field.

I trot up the staircase, weaving between a popcorn seller and a train of Little Leaguers following their coach, and I exit into the corridor, my hands jammed into my jeans' pockets.

I look up, and, unexpectedly, I see Gabrielle ahead of me, leaning against the wall.

She has her hands stuffed in her pockets, too, one leg cocked against the wall. She's wearing the hell out of that pinstripe suit of hers, as if she's the female version of Cary Grant. When she glances at me with a rogueish, sideways smile, she literally takes my breath away, if only for a heartbeat.

"Enjoying the game?" she asks in her sexy, husky voice.

"Yes," I tell her simply, smiling at her.

And then we stand together, everything unsaid between us rising up like a brick wall.

I watch her face for a long moment. She's gazing at me with nothing but affection, her turquoise eyes soft and gentle, but they don't contain the same spark that she showed me last night. I bite my lip, worrying and wondering, and then I curl my hands into fists at my hips, straightening my shoulders.

I'm tired of denying the fact that I have feelings for her. I'm tired of squashing every desire I have when I'm around her. You know what? *She kissed me last night, too,* and, yeah, we haven't had a chance to talk about last night yet, or exactly what it means for us, but whether we talked about it or not doesn't matter.

Because last night, we didn't need any

talking.

All we did was kiss.

And that was enough.

I'm working up the courage to say something, to find the perfect words to convey what I felt last night, what I feel right now, but even though I'm a live reporter, and even though coming up with the perfect phrase at the drop of a hat is kind of my trade, I'm failing. I can't think of the words, the perfect combination, even as I try, desperately, to. And for a long moment, Gabrielle looks as if she wants to say something, too. Her face grows tired, her mouth downturns at the corners, and my heart sinks inside of me. She's going to say something along the lines of, "We can't do this," and, "We have to stop," even though we did nothing more than kiss.

We haven't done anything wrong, either of us. Love should never be forbidden. I don't necessarily know why the rule is in place, angels not being permitted to fall in love with humans, but it seems wrong, somehow. Angels love humans so much that they spend their lives protecting them.

That sounds a lot like love to me.

Gabrielle sighs, jerks her chin back toward the ballfield. "I think you should go back," she says then, and in front of me, just as I blink, she disappears completely.

A woman trots past me, walking into the

bathroom, her Red Sox baseball cap on backwards. She doesn't look like she's surprised that Gabrielle blinked out of existence right in front of her, which means that Gabrielle probably wasn't visible to her. I don't claim to know how this angelic stuff works. I often wonder why, when Gabrielle is invisible, she's still capable of throwing a shadow. But whether I understand it or not, Gabrielle is no longer showing herself to me.

We're going to have to talk later. Now's not the time.

My heart full of confusion, I use the restroom quickly and race back to my seat.

The bases are still loaded. Only a few minutes have passed since I saw Gabrielle, and my heart is as heavy as an anvil.

I realized when I was standing right next to her that I wanted to kiss her again. That it seemed as if no time had passed at all between last night and that moment. I wanted to take her into my arms and kiss her fiercely, the two of us pressing close together, heart to heart, just as easily and effortlessly as we did last night.

I'm so frustrated that all I can do is sigh, crossing my arms in front of me as impotent frustration burns through my chest. I know that the only way to make anything better is to talk to Gabrielle outright about it, but I'm scared that she'll simply break my heart.

Because I'm fairly certain that's what

Gabrielle had been about to do in the hallway.

Suddenly, Ginger sits up beside me a little taller. The loud *crack* of a bat hitting a baseball is echoing in the stadium all around us.

"Oh, shit," Ginger mutters reverently.

The ball is propelled so strongly by that powerful bat hit that it's flying out over the crowd in Fenway Park. This is a foul ball. This is definitely a foul ball, a foul ball that some lucky Red Sox fan is going to be able to take home; then they'll tell everyone the story of how they caught it. But that lucky person is definitely not going to be Ginger. The ball's trajectory is aimed to the right and lower down, probably twenty rows of seats ahead of us, at least. The people below, almost in slow motion, raise their hands or their gloves...

But then the ball does something a little weird...

Or, you know, *suspicious*.

The ball is definitely going to hit low in the bleachers. Now that the ball is closer, I can guess that it's going to land about ten rows down from us. But it...doesn't. Instead, the ball rises a little higher, which isn't physically possible, and it begins to veer *straight toward us*.

I'm staring incredulously at the ball as *Eye of the Tiger* begins to play in my head—appropriate, really. And, in slow motion, Ginger lifts her gloved hand; the ball hurtles toward her determinedly.

And then the ball lands in her glove, almost *leaping* into her palm.

The crowd around us explodes into uproarious applause, the closest people thumping Ginger on the back in excitement as Ginger lifts her glove aloft, holding up the miraculous foul ball, her face beaming with the purest happiness I've ever seen in my life.

Just now, Ginger fulfilled one of her lifelong wishes: she just caught a Red Sox foul ball.

I hug her tightly as Ginger jumps up and down in an uncharacteristic burst of exuberance, the crowd still cheering. And then the stands calm down again, and we all resume our seats. I lean back a little in my chair, turn my head.

"Thanks, Gabrielle. You made her millennium," I whisper beneath my breath, smile tugging at the corners of my mouth.

I feel feathers brush over my cheek as the game plays on.

⌛

The Red Sox win, four to two.

Ginger is so happy that she's hardly able to string together a coherent sentence to express her joy. She just keeps saying things like, "My team!" and, "So proud!" and "My ball!" When she blurts out that last one, she holds the precious foul ball that she caught (thanks to angelic intervention) high in the air. She asked the hot dog vendors for a plastic bag and sealed up the ball inside of it, to "keep it safe," she told me. She's clutching it to her chest now in a pose very reminiscent of a brand-new mother holding a newborn, eyes aglow with unadulterated bliss. I don't think I've ever seen her this happy before.

And it's pretty wonderful.

Ginger drops me off at my apartment with a big, tight hug and a promise to call me tomorrow—ostensibly to "go get a coffee" but more plausibly to wheedle more details out of me about my "new lady love." But, right now, she's going to go home to celebrate the Sox winning (and her acquisition of the mystical, magical foul ball) by drinking herself into an even happier stupor.

I chuckle, hug her one last time, and then climb out of the Jeep and into the warm sunshine of a beautiful summer afternoon.

For a long moment, I hold my face up to the sun. Ginger always keeps the temperature in her Jeep just slightly above freezing, and it feels so good to have this warm light shining down on me, dazzling in the bright blue sky. God, I love summer. It's such a beautiful day, and even though I was outside for the whole Sox game, I feel like I don't want to shut myself up indoors yet. I want to take a walk. There's blood pumping through my veins because of the excitement of the game—sports fan or not, I couldn't help but get excited, sitting next to Ginger with her amped-up enthusiasm for her favorite team—and there's adrenaline running through me, inspired by last night. Though I still don't know what to do about Gabrielle.

Well, speak of the angel... Because when I lower my eyes and look toward my apartment, Gabrielle is sitting on the front steps, waiting for me, elbows on her knee, chin cradled in her hands.

For a long moment, we gaze at one another across the short expanse separating us. There are only a few feet of sidewalk between Gabrielle and me. She shifts, lounging back on the steps, positioning her elbows on the step above her. Her legs are stretched out in front of her, crossed at the ankles, as if she's making herself comfortable, settling in for a long stay on the rough concrete. She breaks eye contact with me and turns her face up to the sunshine; her turquoise eyes are closed as she soaks up the rays.

God, she's beautiful. I let myself feel that awe for a moment, that raw, fierce attraction that burns through me as brightly and warmly as the sunlight pouring down on the both of us, dappling the street with gold, suffusing the space between us with warmth. Her mouth is slightly, slyly tilted, her beautiful, full mouth that I kissed last night. I remember the heat of her, the softness of her lips.

Her eyes are still closed, her long lashes gently resting upon her smooth, high cheekbones, and her hair is settled loosely around her shoulders. I know what her hair feels like, remember the way that the silkiness of it waved through my fingers like water.

I bask in the glow of my desire for her, the strength of it, and then, that longing still burning through me, I know, at last, what I have to do.

It's not going to be easy. But she deserves this. She deserves my honesty, my whole truth.

"Hey," I begin, with a soft smile, walking up to her.

She glances at me, shielding her bright, turquoise gaze against the sun, and offers up a dazzling smile. But there's a tinge of worry behind her expression, I realize, as she rests her gaze upon me. Worry and regret shadowing her lovely face already.

I draw in a deep breath. Wow... This is going to be rough. Painful. I can feel the beginnings of the pain to come lancing through my heart.

"Would you...would you walk with me?", I ask her then, wincing internally at how uncertain I sound. Come *on*, self. You're Erin McEvoy. You interview clowns and bunny breeders with the same grace and aplomb that you would *probably* interview the President of the United States if, you know, you could ever get access to her. You can most certainly talk to an angel about feelings and kisses and...stuff like that.

I take another deep breath, my stomach twisting inside of me.

Right now, right this moment, I don't particular *feel* as if I can talk to Gabrielle about feelings and kisses and stuff like that. But I'm going to have to, anyway. No time like the present. This conversation has to happen—now.

Even though I know, at the very end of my pouring my heart out to her, she's going to tell me that we can't be together, not in the way I want us to be.

"So, the game was good?" asks Gabrielle then, and—as I'm watching her—her pinstripe suit fades away in front of me, changing and morphing into something else entirely. Right now, instead of her normal suit, she's wearing a Red Sox jersey and baseball pants. She shrugs her satiny hair over her shoulders so that it slides down her back.

The pants are hugging her hips and thighs in such a distracting, mesmerizing way that, in that moment, I feel kind of dizzy, unbalanced. I rip my gaze away from her rear as she folds upright gracefully in front of me, and then she begins to walk down the sidewalk, leading the way.

I clear my throat. Then I chuckle a little as she turns around slowly, posing like a confident model at the end of a cat walk.

"Do you like my costume?" she asks mischievously, her voice lilting up at the end of the question, as if she's about to laugh at the expression on my face. But she doesn't.

"I...I do," I tell her, a little breathlessly, clearing my throat again. I feel as if I've just swallowed gravel. We begin to move down the block together, side by side.

Normally, whenever we walk anywhere together, Gabrielle leans toward me and offers me her arm. She smiles a little, her mouth turning up at the corners almost slyly, proudly, as she jabs out her elbow, chin tilted up questioningly.

But, here and now, she doesn't do any of those things. She maintains a constant distance between us. And my heart sinks inside of me. I sigh as we reach the end of the block.

"Gabrielle, we have to talk about what happened last night," I finally say, every word quiet and subdued, as if I'm dredging them up from the very bottom of my soul. I guess that's exactly what I'm doing. But now they're out there, hanging between us.

And it's her move next.

Gabrielle turns to face me, her turquoise eyes narrowed in concern as she searches my gaze. "All right. What do you want to talk about, Erin?" she asks me softly.

I'm highly aware of the fact that I'm

standing on my street in broad daylight on a Saturday. Generally, I'm not a public-displays-of-affection kind of person, but there is so much feeling and raw emotion moving through me right now that I can't stop what happens next.

Gabrielle is looking at me, facing me. Her mouth is open just a little, her lips parted; they're glistening softly, as if she just licked them. She's staring at me with such a soft, attentive gaze, and then I'm leaning toward her, wrapping my hands around her waist, pulling her to me as I hope with every fiber of my being that I'm not wrong, that I've not been wrong about everything, hoping that she doesn't actually regret last night...

All I am, in that moment, is a bright body of hope as I pull the angel toward me, and I kiss her.

Gabrielle's mouth is soft against mine as our lips meet, but for a heartbeat, she doesn't respond. I wonder if she's shocked by my audacity—drawing her close and kissing her like this—but then Gabrielle is reaching up, curling her fingers into the hair at the back of my head, holding me to her, just as I'm holding her to me. And she's kissing me back fiercely, adamantly as she bends against me, my angel's kiss warm and hot and wholly consuming. Just like fire.

Now I know. Now I know, as she kisses me harder, that she does not regret last night, that maybe all of the feelings I'm having for her are reciprocated—if I dare hope as much.

But when we both back away, her lips wetter now, just-kissed and bright pink, I can see the cloudy confusion in her bright turquoise eyes, and anxiety flares in my belly again.

"Erin," she says my name slowly, carefully, letting her hand drop from my hair to my shoulder, then back to her side again. "Erin," she repeats softly, her voice full of regret.

"Yes," I murmur, biting my lip, bracing myself.

"We can't do this," she says then, stepping back, away from me. There's a sudden rush of warm air between our bodies, occupying the space where we were merged before, the two of us pressing so tightly together that it seemed, in that moment, that nothing could possibly pull us apart.

I swallow, feeling my heart dry up and begin to crumble inside of me. "Why can't we?" I ask her then.

She shakes her head, rakes her long fingers back through her hair as she considers me. "It's just not allowed," she says regretfully. "This. Us. Humans and angels can't be together. That's one of the oldest laws, older than time itself."

"But...you have to guard people all the time, right?" I ask, upset at the desperation creeping into my tone. I don't want to be desperate, but I feel, deeply now, that she wants this as much as I do. And some sort of *rule* is going to keep us apart when we both want this, when we want each other? I can't bear that. "If you guard people," I say as reasonably as I can, "you're telling me that this has never happened before? A human falling in love with an angel? I would think it'd happen all the time. I mean...*angels*." I wave my hand helplessly. "They're, like, the greatest things *ever* to the human race, whether someone is religious or not. And I'm fairly certain that we, as a race, wouldn't be able to stop ourselves from falling in love with you guys pretty often."

"Well," says Gabrielle, wincing. "It was unorthodox of me to reveal myself to you."

I stare at her. "It was?"

"Well," she says again, drawing out the word and rocking back on her heels a little, "we're not exactly *supposed* to do that. It's really *supposed* to be the very, very, very..." She counts on her fingers a few times, "*very* last thing we choose to do, as in...the person will definitely die if we don't show ourselves. Which, you know, isn't often..." She's still wincing.

I stare at her, jubilation rising in my heart. "So," I begin, raising a single brow, "you didn't have to reveal yourself to me, but you did. Why, Gabrielle?"

"Because," she says simply, lifting her chin, eyes twinkling, "I wanted to meet you. I wanted to see you and...touch you. I've been...watching you for a long time, Erin. Long enough to learn your patterns and the way you live, in order to predict your dangers. In order to save you. And from the first moment..." She shoves her hands into her pockets. "There was something there." Her mouth turns down a little. "Something very strong. Something I'd never felt before but that came from my gut...even when I didn't have a body," she says, the ghost of a smile on her face. But the ghost vanishes, and a frown returns.

"But I've thought a lot about it," she whispers then, reaching out and curling her fingers around my upper arms. She holds them gently as she stares down into my eyes. "And it's true: I don't honestly know if a human has ever fallen for an angel before, but it has never happened to the best of my knowledge. There aren't any stories about it among my kind. We never speak of such things because it's...well, it's forbidden. And we don't speak of forbidden things." She holds my gaze.

"But *why*?" I ask her. "*Why* is it forbidden?"

Gabrielle shrugs. "There is no *why*. We're not told why we can or can't do anythings. We simply do as we're told," she says, jaw clenching as she lets go of me, her hands returning to her sides. "Well, that makes it sound awful. It's not really as bad as all that. We do love what we do. Our jobs are the most important thing to us," she whispers. "It's...why we were created."

"All right. But I don't understand how this"—I motion between us—"can possibly be considered wrong," I tell her plaintively, and she looks so pained as she lifts her chin and meets my gaze.

"It's not wrong, Erin. Not as you define the word. There's a difference between *wrong* and *forbidden*."

"Why the *hell* would something be forbidden if it's not considered wrong?" I ask her, practically spluttering. It makes no sense to me; I'm nearly rendered speechless.

Gabrielle, again, shrugs. "I don't know."

"*Argh*," I sigh, and then I turn around and begin to pace up and down the sidewalk, right in front of her, taking deep breaths and trying to detangle my thoughts. "I hope you know," I say huffily, as I spin back on my heel, "angelic law is illogical."

Gabrielle watches me, her lips faintly curving up at the corners, but she doesn't actually smile. "It's not supposed to make sense," she says then, with another shrug. "Not to humans, anyway," she tells me, her head tilted to one side.

I pause. And I take another deep breath. "Okay," I tell her in a calm, reasonable tone. "So what happens if you *do* fall in love with a human? What's the consequence?"

Gabrielle's gaze softens as she looks deep

inside of me, holding my gaze like she holds my hands now, reaching out across the space between us and scooping them up into her palms, squeezing them tightly.

"We fall," she tells me, searching my gaze.

"Like...like a fallen angel," I murmur, dredging up everything I know about fallen angels...which isn't a whole lot, just crumbs gleaned from pop culture. "And what does it mean to be a fallen angel?" I search her face as she turns away from me, closing her eyes, working her jaw.

"I don't know," she whispers, her voice so soft that I can hardly hear her. Gabrielle lifts her chin, gazes back at me. "Because it's never happened, that I know of," she says carefully. "But, like I told you, we don't speak of forbidden things."

"Gabrielle," I breathe, that one simple, beautiful word filled with so much longing that I can feel my heart aching inside of me, just from saying it.

To fall. Angels *fly*. The word "fall" is probably the worst one they could think of in their vocabulary.

Gabrielle hasn't released my hands yet, and she squeezes them again—tightly. "Erin," she whispers, and she draws in a breath to say something else, but the cell phone in my purse starts ringing.

I turned my personal cell phone off

during the ballgame, but I couldn't turn off my work phone. I'm on-call today, and on the off-chance that there aren't enough news reporters available, I am assigned to fill in.

I frown a little, frustrated that we're being interrupted from this conversation, this very important conversation, as I pull the phone from my purse and stare down at the screen.

"Sorry. I'll only be a minute," I tell Gabrielle, who nods, shifting away from me, shoving her hands into her pockets, her jaw still clenched. She wants to talk, too, and we need to figure this out before the day is over.

I sigh and answer the call. "Hey, Scott," I say into the phone. "What's up?"

"Hey!" he replies, but I can hardly hear him, because there are so many sirens blaring in the background. "Listen, Erin, there's a police chase happening right now, right in downtown Boston if you'd believe it, and the station manager asked *us* to cover it. Isn't that crazy?" I can hear the excitement in his voice, despite the still-trumpeting sirens. "Apparently, he was pretty impressed by our work with the chimpanzee story, and he wants to see if we can handle, and I quote, 'real news.'" He chuckles. "Anyway, where are you?"

"At my apartment," I tell him, glancing at Gabrielle with wide eyes.

Police chase? Well, that sounds pretty dangerous and life-threatening.

Is this...*it*? Is this the thing that Gabrielle is supposed to save me from, whatever it is that's about to happen today? I feel sick to my stomach with worry—not because my life is possibly in danger (okay, partially because of that), but with the very real fear that the moment my life is spared, Gabrielle is going to, somehow, disappear from my life. Because her mission will be over, and she'll be spirited away to her next task, to be the guardian angel of someone else.

And she will leave. And I'll never be able to find her again...

"Erin?"

"Oh, sorry," I tell Scott, swallowing as I shake my head at myself. "What did you say?" I grip the phone tightly.

"Can you get here? It's only about four blocks from your apartment, I think." He gives me the address, and I lift my head, glancing down the street. It's actually five blocks away, and I vaguely recall hearing faint sirens in the distance... Gabrielle and I could get to the scene in a few minutes, if we walked very fast.

"Yeah, I'll be right there," I tell him, my mouth dry as I hang up my phone. I stare at Gabrielle for a long moment. Her eyes are dark, and there is no hint of a smile on that beautiful, angelic face. She already knows something is wrong. I wonder if she, too, feels that something significant is about to happen, the something that she was sent here to prevent...

I push the thought from my mind. Denial is my only coping mechanism right now.

"That was Scott," I tell Gabrielle hoarsely, sliding the phone into my purse with clammy hands. "There's a car chase, um, involving the police, and they want us, Scott and me, to cover it..." I lift my eyes to seek out her gaze. She staring at me intensely. I swallow. "Do you think this is... I mean, do you think this might be the time when I'm supposed to..." Heart hammering, I draw in a deep breath. "Do you think I might die today?"

Gabrielle's jaw clenches, and she lifts her chin. But she doesn't say a word.

And that answers my question.

I turn, and together, side by side, we walk down the sidewalk again, much more quickly than before.

But this time, Gabrielle reaches across the space between us to grasp my hand. She gently takes it and threads it through the crook of her arm, just as she's always done, since the very first day that I met her. A little thrill jump-starts my heart, and I allow myself a small moment of realization. Yes, Gabrielle told me that falling in love with a human is forbidden, and neither of us knows, exactly, what that means, but she also said that, from the first moment she saw me...there was a spark. Something that she felt for me.

And that she still feels now.

That's important. That's crucial, because while I don't know if we can be together, the connection between us is still a sacred thing.

All of my life, I've wanted a soul-deep connection with someone, a strong, lasting connection. I've wanted the type of love that made your heart ache or rise inside of you whenever you thought about that beloved person. And I think I'm beginning to have a taste of it.

No matter what happens today, no matter what happens tomorrow, right here, right now, Gabrielle is holding my arm tightly, and I know that she's falling in love with me just as much as I'm falling in love with her.

And this one tiny, perfect moment is enough to keep my feet going, taking step after step toward what might possibly be the moment of my death.

It's a weird sensation, as we make our way toward the police barricade that I can just begin seeing down the street. I might, really and truly, die today.

I think that would be a weird sensation for *anybody* to experience.

There are people gathered, milling on the sidewalks, and the traffic comes to a standstill the further along we go, until we reach a jumble of news vans, the BEAN's news van hovering on the very outskirts.

I stop then, realizing with surprise that Gabrielle is still visible—at least to me. Is she visible to other people? But then a guy walks past us, and he moves around her, which must means that she is, in fact, visible. Which...isn't normal.

She catches my expression and smiles a little, with a nonchalant shrug, but I can't help noticing that the smile doesn't quite reach her eyes. "I have to stay visible this time," she says, her jaw tight. "Just..." She watches me carefully. "Just in case. I've got to be able to get to you in time and, well, do whatever it takes." She squeezes my arm a little before she lets it go.

I swallow as Scott waves us over from his spot, holding his camera aloft, leaning against the van. My legs are stiff as we make our way over to him, but I can't stop moving. I have to do this. And Gabrielle is here. I feel safe, knowing that she's here.

But still, I have to be realistic and realize that there's a possibility that I might die soon. If Gabrielle can't save me in time...

I shake my head. My lungs feel tight; I can only take shallow breaths.

"Really?" Scott chuckles when I get closer, glancing down at my Red Sox wear, and I chuckle a little, too, even though laughing is really the last thing I want to be doing right now. I clear my throat, stand aside and gesture to Gabrielle.

"Scott, this is my..." I falter. Oh, crap. What *is* Gabrielle to me? My friend? My girlfriend? We've certainly never talked about girlfriend status, but she more or less declared, by word and action, that she was drawn to me as much as I'm drawn to her...

God, this is *not* the time or place to be grappling with this, but it's somehow important to me.

Scott is staring, and so is Gabrielle, but her mouth is curling up at the corners.

"This is my girlfriend Gabrielle," I finally say, almost shouting it to be heard over the blaring sirens. And then I don't skip a beat as Gabrielle begins to smile truly, a bright, dazzling smile that takes my breath away. "And, Gabrielle," I say, clearing my throat, "this is Scott. He's a great friend, and the best cameraman in the city."

Scott grins hugely and holds out his hand to Gabrielle, who takes it with a soft smile; they shake.

Introducing Scott to my guardian angel feels really weird, admittedly. Taking into account, every day, that Gabrielle is not a normal human being...that's a strange realization, and I keep having it over and over again every moment that we're together.

But it's also pretty wonderful, introducing such an important part of my life—Scott—to Gabrielle. It makes all of this feel so much more real. And introducing Gabrielle as my *girlfriend* felt radical, crazy. An angel! My girlfriend!

As they shake hands, I can feel Gabrielle gaining more substance in my life, even as the possibility of her departure looms on the horizon.

Literally. Because Scott jerks his chin toward the street and the little bit of hill that the police have set up a blockade in front of, about three squad cars deep, their lights flashing, the sirens occasionally blaring, but also turned off from time to time as they talk among themselves.

"Nice to meet you," Scott says quickly to Gabrielle; then he points to the squad cars. "You guys got here just in time. The whole brigade is going to be coming over the hill in a couple of seconds. See, the barricade is set up right there, so the chase is going to end soon, one way or the other."

One way or the other. It's the most ominous grouping of words I've ever heard in my life.

Suddenly, nerves consume me, and I realize that my hands are shaking. It isn't every day that you're confronted with the possibility of death. *This might be the moment I die.* It's unnerving, and I'm starting to feel a little lightheaded as Scott hands me a microphone, as I turn to make my way toward the barricade, inching between the gathered people and the other news reporters. Scott follows closely behind me, and after him comes Gabrielle. I keep turning around to see if she's still there, and of course she is, but as we reach the barricade, she folds seamlessly into the crowd, prowling among the people like a lioness, scouting out the area. She finds a spot about five feet away and plants herself there, arms folded in front of her, as she watches me closely.

"Okay," I tell Scott, turning to him. "What do we know?"

"The chase started about an hour ago, and the guy keeps making big blocks because he's trying to get out of the city, but he's been barricaded in with every attempt. We don't know his motivation, but the police have been herding him to this spot," says Scott. "Good?"

I nod. I'm not "good" at all, but I have to do this, so here goes nothing.

"Five, four," says Scott; then he holds up his fingers as we switch to the live feed. He lifts his camera. Three...two...one...

My heart is fluttering in my chest as I try my best to look serious, not nervous — because nerves don't look great on camera. I draw in a deep breath, lifting my microphone. "This is Erin McEvoy with BEAN at the scene of the car chase currently happening in the heart of Boston." Somehow I manage to force the words out.

Behind me, the lines of police squad cars

turn on their deafening sirens, and as Scott moves the focus off of me, pointing the camera behind us, I glance over my shoulder too, looking at the policemen waiting to capture the suspect. All of them are armed, poised behind their vehicles with guns at the ready, pointed toward the empty street.

And that's when it happens.

The car crests the little hill and starts to advance toward the squad cars. The chased car is small, but it's very fast, the black, shiny vehicle streaking toward the line of police cars as if it actually thinks it can break through them all. But I know it can't. I've seen a couple of other chases end like this; the police have staggered their vehicles three deep across the width of the perimeter, which means that you're not going to be able to get through it unless you're driving something much, much bigger. Possibly a Hummer could break through the squad car barricade. But this little black car doesn't stand a chance.

That doesn't seem to deter the driver at all.

I thought we were set up back far enough that, if anything happened involving the car and the police cruisers set up in the barricade, we'd still be safe. That's what all of the other news reporters did. After all, we report the news; we don't want to become part of it. But as the car crests the hill, and as I see all of the police cars chasing after it like angry bees, I take in the whole scene—the speed of the car, the police cruisers in the barricade and all of the other police cars giving chase...

And my very bad feeling escalates.

I take a deep breath, and then it happens, just like that. The car hits the police cars.

It happens so fast, actually, that I can't even breathe as the deafening sound of the cars crunching together explodes in the air. There are pieces of cars flying up into the sky slowly, almost, arcing gracefully, and then the rest of the world catches up. There weren't any policemen or women behind the first line of police cars that the chased car hit, so at least they're safe. But the car is still moving, and so are all of the cars that it hit...

Everything, suddenly, is moving too fast. The cars, the people scrambling to get out of the way. Scott, to his credit, keeps the camera trained on the scene as he starts to walk backwards very, very quickly, but everyone is moving; all of the people who were trying to catch a glimpse of the action, and all of the reporters and their camera crews, are trying to move away from the trajectory of that car...

"Gabrielle?" I call out as the first scream finally fills the air. "Gabrielle?"

But she's right there, her fingers curling around my upper arm, tense and ready to spring into action to do whatever she needs to do to fix the situation...

But it doesn't need fixing.

There are only a few screams, and they die down almost instantly. Everyone is getting out of the way with more than enough time, and gravity is working, dragging the crumpled hulk of the chased car to a halt. Everyone stops, then immediately turns their cameras back onto the car, waiting for the suspect to emerge, if able.

And the guy does emerge. He rolls down the tinted window of his driver's side and crawls out through the window as the police call out for him to put his hands up, to lie down on the ground. The suspect is wearing all black, and he looks like he's maybe eighteen, nineteen, and in way, way over his head, his face paling as he stares at all of the people around him, as he stares at the policemen with their guns trained on him. He looks like a rich kid who possibly took a dare that got very out of control. The little black car that now resembles a tin can? It's an expensive model—or...was.

The suspect is obedient, and the whole situation is quiet, peaceful as the policemen put him in handcuffs, reading him his rights as he winces while they pull his arms behind him.

"Well," I tell the camera, holding up the microphone, "there don't appear to be any serious injuries, just from witnessing the events here today. We will have more information for you as we learn more. This is Erin McEvoy,

BEAN News."

Scott maintains the camera on the suspect but cuts the feed, and I let my microphone fall as we watch the policeman above the suspect yelling at him. The suspect is wincing on the ground.

"That was easy," says Gabrielle, curling her fingers tighter around my arm. Her hand is so warm, so reassuring, and I'm weak with relief. An elegant frown causes Gabrielle's lips to swoop downward, and she sighs through her nose. "So I guess that wasn't...*it*," she says, glancing at me, her eyes trailing my length. I can feel a flush on my cheeks as she very carefully examines me. "You're all right?" she asks, voice low as she reaches out and gently traces her fingertips down my arm to cup my elbow. She draws me a little closer to her.

"Yeah," I tell her, feeling my heart flutter inside of me, beating against my rib cage like it wants to get out. I glance up at her, clear my throat. "I'm going to go talk to the police, try to see if I can get some information for the late report..."

She glances away, considering the situation, which has already resolved itself, but then she nods reluctantly. "I'll come with you," she says softly

Scott follows after the two of us but stays back, still taking video footage of the man on the ground, of the police hauling him upward. This footage will probably be used tonight when they run the story again, this time with more information about the suspect and his motivation... Information that I need to get now. I also need to see if I can extract a statement from the police—something they generally don't like doing for the press.

Now that the immediate threat is past, my legs feel a little bit like overcooked noodles, the used-up adrenaline leaking out of me, leaving me exhausted. But still, I lift my chin. I'm usually pretty good at wheedling a few words out of the police, and the ones closest to the car seem to be loitering around, not doing much, which hopefully means this will be easy. I make a beeline for them.

"Excuse me, sir," I say to the closest one, an older guy wearing sunglasses and a frown. "Do you have a second for just a question or two?"

He turns to me with the most bored-looking expression possible. He glances down at my Red Sox jersey and then looks away. "You're in a crime scene, lady," he drawls. "Get the hell out of here."

I'm not deterred. I make my smile bigger. "Do you know why the suspect was fleeing the scene of..." I pause.

"A 7-Eleven," Scott prompts helpfully from behind me.

"The 7-Eleven?" I ask the police with

what is, hopefully, my biggest, most captivating smile *ever*.

The cop shrugs, turning back to his car, crossing his arms in front of him.

I try the guy next to him.

"Excuse me, sir," I begin again...

But everything around me stops at that moment.

Because the crumpled, smoking car, the chased car that was simply sitting there, crisis averted...

Explodes.

The vehicle had hit the police cars pretty hard, and its nose was certainly squished, but there were no telltale signs of imminent explosion, no scent of gas in the air... One minute, the car was sitting there, crunched and gently smoking but still, and the next, there's glass everywhere, metal debris flying into the sky, and everyone close by is blown backward, including me.

Actually, no. I'm not blown backward.

I'm *flown* backward.

Gabrielle is right in front of me, holding me tightly, scooping her arms around my shoulders and under my knees and lifting me in the blink of an eye. Then her wings are out, unfurling into the air with such a poignant *snap* that the sound alone would have taken my breath away if the exploding car hadn't. Her wings are bright and white as they rise over us, around us, keeping us safe. Gabrielle is in the air so fast that I can't focus on her movements, and she flies me away from the exploding car in a heartbeat. In fact, she soars me straight down the street, safely out of harm's way.

After she sets me, very gently, on the ground, the first thing that I can think about is Scott, but he's taken cover behind one of the police cars and appears to be safe.

The two cops that had been standing beside the police car are miraculously unharmed, too.

In fact...

I stop and stare, my heart pounding inside of me. Because the cop who hadn't wanted to talk to me is in the arms of a guy — a tall guy. A guy wearing a white suit... A guy who has *wings*. Enormous wings, wings that are just as big as Gabrielle's, wings that are bright white, practically glowing, stretching overhead and then unfurling around the two of them.

But even as I notice this man and his gigantic wings, he seems to disappear right in front of me, as if he were there one moment, and then completely gone the next, which leaves the rescued cop with his mouth hanging open, stunned, as he stares back at the wreckage of the exploded car, and the wreckage of the police car he'd been standing next to, now in countless pieces, burning in the street.

That cop, like me, should be dead.

But he isn't.

An angel saved him. And I *saw* it happen.

In that moment, I'm speechless with awe. I mean, how many times do angels save us every day, and we don't know it, recognize it, or see it? How many times are horrible things supposed to happen, but they just...don't? How many times are we supposed to die, but we don't—because someone is watching out for us?

Beside me, Gabrielle reaches out with both arms, and then I'm pressed tightly against her, her arms wrapped so tightly around me that I can hardly breathe. But I'm holding her just as tightly, too, burying my face against the curve of her shoulder and neck. I breathe in the scent of her, the sweet, earthy scent of my angel, while the realization that I should be dead but am, in fact, *not* dead courses through me.

But then, just as quickly, comes the realization that Gabrielle just saved my life. She saved my life, absolutely. I should be mortally wounded, but I'm alive, uninjured...

And that means that it's over. Gabrielle's mission is over.

And Gabrielle will have to go.

I look up at her, and she's staring down at me with such wide, beautiful turquoise eyes. My heart beats so fast, and I'm filled with so much emotion, so much longing and frustration, and—hell—even rage that it has to end like this. That she has to go, that what we had between us will be snuffed out before it could even really flare.

I don't want her to go.

God, I *don't want her to go*.

But even as that raw want roars through me, I can see the flicker of something odd in Gabrielle's eyes. Her expression changes, in that instant, from pure relief to pure sadness...

And then she bends down, and Gabrielle presses a kiss to my mouth. But this isn't like the kiss from last night. Last night, it was hot, sure, full of passion and the bliss of tasting her for the very first time.

But this time, this kiss, it's so much *more*. It's full of raw, true want, and she kisses me so hard, so deeply that I can feel us merging together, heart to heart, mouth to mouth; she drinks me in so deeply that all that I am is connected, utterly, to this angel in my arms. We hold each other tightly, like lifelines, like we're never going to let go. As if holding each other could keep Gabrielle here with me on Earth. But I don't think that I can hold her here. Not if she's drawn back, absent of free will. And she will be drawn back, I know, an ache rising in me. She must be taken back to her home, because her mission with me is through.

Gabrielle tastes sweet—sweet and soft and warm. And then, I realize, she tastes salty too, because one hot tear traces its way down her cheek and falls between our lips. And I taste it.

I taste her sadness.

Gabrielle backs away, still holding onto me.

She looks up at the sky. And then she looks back down at me. There is so much bare emotion on her face, so much that she isn't saying, but I can feel it, anyway.

"I almost lost you," Gabrielle says, her words low and thick as she chokes them out. She repeats them again, holding me tighter. "I almost *lost* you," she growls out, and then she's shaking her head as she presses me to her, encircling me with the warmth of her arms, with the warmth of all that she is as she places her chin on the top of my head, holding me close, rocking me side to side gently, tenderly. "I... It's unthinkable," she says, her voice catching. "I can't imagine losing you. I can't imagine a world without you in it," she whispers.

My heart overflows inside of me, but—at the same time—it's breaking, too, breaking into small, fragile pieces. In the short time we've been together, I've acknowledged (at least to myself) that I'm falling in love with Gabrielle, that—from the first moment I met her—I knew that I was attracted to her, that there was something between the angel and me that I couldn't exactly place or name but recognized all the same. There was a bond, and it was unbreakable.

And now, here, Gabrielle is staring down

at me with such a fierce light in her eyes. I'd hoped, so much, that she felt the same way about me.

She whispers, "Erin," and the way she says my name sounds like a prayer, like that word is cherished. "Erin," she repeats, her voice breaking, "*I can't imagine a world without you in it,*" she says, and her eyes are wide, her turquoise eyes so bright, so blue as they're washed in tears. "And there's nowhere else I'd rather be than by your side."

My heart skips in my chest. Then Gabrielle's eyes turn stormy, and she looks up at the sky again.

"Do you hear me?" she shouts up to the sky, and I'm speechless for a moment as she takes a step closer to me. I'm pressed against her again, her arms wrapped tightly around me. "Do you *hear* me?" she repeats, shouting. I can feel the rumble of the words in her chest as she lifts her head to the heavens; her voice practically makes the ground shake: "There's nowhere else I'd rather be than by her side," she says, and then her voice deepens a little more as she shouts upward, "I love her! I love a human!" Her voice is purely unapologetic, resplendent and triumphant. It defies the sky, her voice.

And then, panting, Gabrielle lowers her gaze and looks at me now.

We stare at one another for a long

moment, saying absolutely nothing. And then, my heart knocking loudly against my bones, I reach up and wrap my arms around her neck, twining my fingers in her satiny brown hair.

I kiss her fiercely, drinking her in, feeling tears spring up to the corners of my eyes but not letting them shed.

An angel just shouted to the heavens that she loves me, defying a forbidding law that's apparently as old as the universe.

My guardian angel did this. My Gabrielle.

She loves me.

So we kiss each other gently, wholeheartedly, and then Gabrielle simply holds me close, tucking her chin on top of my head, wrapping her arms around me tightly.

I don't know if we're visible to the other people surrounding us, but even if we are, there's so much chaos that no one's paying attention to us. No one even looked our way when Gabrielle shouted, because *everyone's* shouting. I'm learning from bits and pieces of shouted words that there was a bomb in the suspect's car.

But none of that matters now. Gabrielle holds me, and I hold her, and the two of us stand together, entwined.

And we wait.

My heart is pounding inside of me. We're waiting for Gabrielle to...what? Disappear? For a fiery horde of angels to appear and declare that Gabrielle was the first angel in recorded history to fall in love with a human, and now she must endure strange and unusual punishment because of that fact?

I don't know what we're waiting for, but it's pretty unnerving.

"Did they hear you?" I ask Gabrielle then, glancing up at her with worry. Whoever *they* are. Angels. Heaven. Whatever. I take a deep breath, but the singed air catches in my throat.

"I don't know," says Gabrielle with a small frown. But then she looks down at me, her smile turning up a little bit at the corners. "But...have you noticed?" She cocks an eyebrow at me and winks. "I'm still here."

We stare at one another.

"You're still here," I repeat, a tiny bit of the tension leaving my shoulders. "But..." I narrow my eyes. "Doesn't that mean that... But you *saved my life*," I tell her, and she shrugs a little.

If Gabrielle was supposed to save my life from the exploding car, that would mean that her mission was over, and she would be taken back home.

But Gabrielle is still here.

"Okay. So what exactly *does* that mean?" I ask her weakly, even though I already know the answer to the question.

"It means that, yet again, that wasn't what

I was supposed to save you from," says Gabrielle, her mouth curling into a soft smile as she shakes her head of shining brown hair. "Something *else* is supposed to happen. Seriously, though," she whispers softly, teasingly, "are you *always* this accident prone?"

I laugh out loud, and then relief floods my entire body, and I'm suddenly weak in the knees. I breathe out slowly. "No. Not usually. Only lately."

She brushes my hair back from my cheek.

"And that's good, I guess, my still needing to be saved," I murmur, because it's true. It isn't exactly my favorite thing in the world, knowing that my life is apparently still in jeopardy, but it's wonderful (more wonderful than I could ever articulate) to know that Gabrielle is sticking around, at least for a little while longer.

"Gabrielle," I whisper, holding her hands tightly, "did you... I mean..." I tilt my head, staring at her in wonder. "What you said," I whisper, trailing off.

"I love you," she says quietly, simply, as she weaves her fingers through mine. "I love you, and I don't care who knows it. I don't know what will happen, but...until something *does* happen, until I'm punished, until I *fall*," she whispers, her jaw tightening, "I'm going to try this. With you." She smiles down at me. "If you're willing."

"I'm willing," I say so quickly that we both laugh softly. Then Gabrielle wraps her arms around me.

"Erin, I've never felt love before," she says, almost reverently. "Oh, I've seen it in plenty of movies, in plenty of lives, and I thought that I really understood what it was, to love, for two people to fall into *love* together, to experience *love* together. But I never *really* knew. I had no idea, not really," she says, laughing a little. She sounds elated, overjoyed. "But now there's you. And everything," she whispers, brushing her lips against the top of my head, flooding me with warmth, "everything has changed."

I close my eyes, sealing this moment away in my memory forever. It's not a moment you'd particularly think you'd want to dredge up again. In the distance, there's a smoking, exploded wreck of a car. There are police sirens blaring everywhere, people shouting, pure chaos. But no one's hurt; everything's okay...

And, really, right now, right here, everything is very much *more* than okay. Because I am in the arms of my angel.

And it's beautiful, this. All of this.

"So," I tell her then, mischievously, smiling in relief. "This has never happened before, *seriously*?" I ask her, wrapping my arms around her neck and standing on my tiptoes. I kiss the side of her mouth like she kissed mine, days ago now, chastely, with a sly smile. "An angel has never fallen in love with a human? Because," I tell her, kissing her again, this time full on her mouth, "I really," another kiss, "really," another kiss, "*really*," a long, lingering kiss...

We come up for air, and I pant a little, leaning against her.

"I *really* find that hard to believe," I finally tell her, grinning. "If all of the other angels are like you."

"Well," says Gabrielle slowly, carefully, and she chuckles against me, "like I told you, I don't know. But it *does* seem as if it might have happened more than once, right? Since the beginning of time? Doesn't quite make sense to me. But I don't know what happened to those hypothetical people and angels who fell in love." Her jaw tightens again, but she relaxes against me with a shrug. "No matter if we are the first," she murmurs into my hair, "or the thousandth or more...we are together right now. This moment, *right now*..."

I take a deep breath. It's been a whirlwind of a day. One to remember.

I realize, as I see Scott walking toward us, looking a little dazed, that I still haven't gotten the information I need from the police, but I'm fairly certain the station will understand. They can pick up what they need from the wire. At least everyone's safe, including Scott. I'm about to ask him if he's really all right as he reaches us, but then he stops, his eyes narrowing as he stares in our direction.

"How are you..." he splutters; then he shakes his head a little. "I'm so glad you're all right," he tells me incredulously, looking me up and down as he lowers the camera from his shoulder. "But...but how is that possible, Erin?" he asks me, shaking his head again. "I mean, I *saw* you. You were right by that police officer, right *next* to him, and then you just...weren't. It's like you flew across the street," he says, chuckling a little at his own words, but his eyes are as wide and wondering as if he'd just seen a ghost.

"Yeah," I say carefully. "Gabrielle...saved me," I tell him, which is truer than he possibly knows. I glance up at Gabrielle, who tightens her hold around my waist.

"Well, I'm glad you're all right," says Scott, looking a little dazed. "And I'm really happy for you guys," he says then, cracking a huge smile, "but this has been kind of a crazy day, and look at what happened." He lifts up his camera to show me the lens: there's a gigantic piece of metal, black metal, in the center of the glass, shattered by the bit of debris. "This thing's shot, so I think I'm going to call it a day," he tells me, raising a brow. "And I think you should, too, you know, before anything *else* happens." He smiles wryly. "You're awfully lucky," says Scott then.

"Yeah," I tell him, squeezing Gabrielle tightly. "I am."

Chapter 6: Seize the Fish

We get home, and I walk Sawyer quickly. My mind is going a million miles a minute. What if I walk Sawyer and walk back up into my apartment, and it's just...empty? What if Gabrielle has disappeared because whoever was supposed to be watching out for angels doing "forbidden" things finally caught up with her and has taken her? Is that how this works? Neither of us *knows* how this works, so anxiety makes my belly churn as I hope against hope that Sawyer can do her potty business as quickly as possible.

But when we return to the apartment, Gabrielle is still there, two grilled cheese sandwiches frying side by side in the pan on the stove. She turns to me with a mischievous smile and flips the pan into the air, the sandwiches flying out of it and landing neatly in the center.

"I've gotten better at cooking since watching over you," says Gabrielle, with a little chuckle. "What do you think? Do I have what it takes for my own cooking show?"

The sandwiches are browning a little too much as she looks at me, so I chuckle and shake my head; smoke begins to billow up from the pan. "I don't know if you're cooking show material yet, Julia Child," I tease her.

"Hmm," says Gabrielle, her head to the side as she considers the now-smoking grilled cheese sandwiches. "These things burn at the drop of a feather," she says, and then she's shifting the frying pan over to an unlit burner and turning off the stove.

"Well," she says then, still holding my gaze with her smoldering eyes. She reaches behind her back and undoes the ties of the apron very slowly, the ties falling to rest against her hips. She lifts the apron over her head and sets it on the counter, holding my gaze the entire time.

"What did you have in mind for the evening?" she asks, her voice a low growl. Every word is spoken so pointedly that my breathing is now coming *very* fast. I'm practically panting as we stand, staring at one another, waiting, tensed...

And then I make my move. I prowl around the kitchen island into the kitchen itself, and when I reach her, I curl my fingers around Gabrielle's hips, my entire body electrified as I feel her hot skin through the fabric of her pants. Without any further ado I press her against the counter, pressing against her, too.

And I kiss her.

That's all it takes. In an instant, the

kitchen—already hot from the frying of the sandwiches—gets a hell of a lot hotter as Gabrielle turns smoothly, taking my hips and pressing them against the counter now, as we move almost as if we're dancing. She's still kissing me, breathing fast now, as I wrap my arms around her neck. And then my bottom isn't pressing against the counter anymore. Instead, I'm being lifted, lifted up and onto the counter, with the cheese and the open bread bag next to me; I push both back, already unbuttoning Gabrielle's pinstripe suit jacket with almost shaking fingers.

Everything's moving so fast, and it's a whirlwind of wonder, of hot, rampant need as I peel the jacket off of her, instantly going for the buttons of her shirt as she reaches up, stroking her fingertips lightly over the curve of my shoulder, cupping her hand at the back of my neck as she pulls me to her. My legs are wrapped around her middle now, and I work furiously at the buttons, want and need pouring through me at such an incandescent rate that my entire body feels like it's on fire.

The need crescendos within me, and it pools into my center as I press against Gabrielle, as Gabrielle's kisses now move to my jaw, down my neck, and she's pulling the Red Sox jersey up and over my head in a quick, graceful move. Even with all of the desire she's showing me right now, everything about Gabrielle is still graceful, is still beautiful, because all that Gabrielle *is* is grace and beauty.

I need her. I need her *now*.

I've never had sex on the counter. Okay, that's not exactly true. I had sex on the counter once with one of my exes, but we spent the whole time saying things like, "We should move to the bedroom," and, "This is kind of awkward, isn't it?" That last one was her, and it makes me wince to remember it, interspersed with nervous laughter, because I really *did* want to move it to the bedroom, and it certainly *was* kind of awkward. You've got to want sex terribly to have it on the counter; you've got to be full of need, desperate and wanting enough to throw the inherent humor of the situation — like, are we really going to have sex next to the loaf of bread? — out the window and focus entirely, instead, on the other person and how much you need them.

But, here and now, that's exactly what's happening. There's nothing but that beautiful longing pulsing between us. When Gabrielle picks me up a little, pulling my jeans down my legs and off of me, I settle back down on the counter and wrap my legs so tightly around her that all I can feel is that press of her hips against my center, and, my God, it feels so *good*. But not good enough. Not what I need, and I need it so desperately.

But Gabrielle seems to know, intuitively,

what I want, as her kisses grow more aggressive, more demonstrative, kisses that contain teeth and tongue as she covers my breasts with her hands, tracing her thumb roughly over the cups of my bra and against the skin she finds there. I shudder against her, and her hands are behind me then; with one expert motion, she undoes the clasp of my bra, dragging the straps over my shoulders as she trails a hot, wet kiss down my arm.

"Are you sure you've never done this before?" I ask her, panting, as she tosses the bra over her shoulder.

"I'm a fast learner," is all she says against my skin, as she drags her fingernails up my thigh, and I shiver.

The last button on her shirt is undone, and I push the shirt off of her, dragging it down her arms and watching it fall to the floor in a flutter of white, like feathers.

She wasn't wearing a bra beneath her shirt. Her breasts are small, perfect, high and round, her nipples bright pink and peaked, and I ache, so much, to kiss them, to taste them, but Gabrielle curls her fingers over my hips and drags me to her, so that my hips and her hips now, are deliciously pressed together. She's still wearing her suit pants, and all I'm wearing are panties, so I shiver as she presses against me, almost experimentally, looking down between us as she pants, her shoulders rising and falling with every breath, her bare shoulders that I can't help but touch. I reach forward, kissing. Her skin is hot beneath my mouth.

And then Gabrielle moves her right hand, tracing the curve where my hips meet my thigh, down, down, moving aside the soaking fabric of my panties.

She's not looking down between us anymore. She's watching me closely, her eyes narrowed a little, her wet mouth parted, panting, as she holds my gaze.

She slowly, almost reverently, brushes the pad of her thumb against my clit, her fingers grazing my slit.

I shudder as she slides her thumb gently over my clit again and again, back and forth, her fingers curling up and into me just a little, just her first two fingertips.

"You're so wet," she murmurs wonderingly. "For me," she says now, her voice in a growl. "For me," she repeats, bending her beautiful head and brushing her lips over my shoulder.

And then she presses her fingers inside of me.

"Yes," is the only syllable I'm capable of saying at that moment. Because everything is *yes*. All that I am is *yes, yes, yes*, as Gabrielle lowers her face now to my breasts, and I arch back as much as I'm able, resting my head against the cabinets as I try to raise my chest to her, asking, begging with the language of my body, for her to kiss me, every inch of me.

Her mouth trails kisses to my right breast, and all she does at first is circle my nipple, drawing kisses in until she draws my nipple into her mouth, biting down against it gently at first. I like it a little rough, a little hard, bites and nips on my breasts, and that's what Gabrielle gives me, as if she knows every inch of my body already. I don't know how she knows, but Gabrielle is flicking her tongue against my nipple, drawing it into her mouth, biting down gently, rocking my nipple against her teeth with her tongue.

I arch against her, whimpering a little as her fingers reach farther, higher, curling in me, and then moving in and out, curling up and in each time, pressing inside of me like an explosion of feeling that makes my toes curl.

I rock my hips against her, and we settle into a quick, hard rhythm of her kissing my breasts, her left hand curling around my hips so hard there's going to probably be a delicious bruise there tomorrow. My legs are wrapped so tightly around her that we move together, and when her thumb quickens its pace against my clit, I'm almost seeing stars, it feels so good. My eyes roll back, I grip the edge of the counter, and I balance entirely against her as she holds me, holds me tightly, safe and euphoric as she draws me closer to bliss.

The first shudder of orgasm moves through me, and stars really do explode behind my vision, because, at that moment, Gabrielle lifts her head and places a kiss on my mouth this time. Her tongue is in my mouth, and she's demonstrative, yes, but as she kisses me deeply, soundly, as she rocks her hand against me, inside of me, I know that I've drawn all of this out of her. My want and her want are inextricably entwined, as entwined as our two bodies are right now, merged utterly.

The orgasm floods through me, and I'm crying out, the swell of euphoria moving through me in perfect, undulating waves, as Gabrielle does not let up, as she presses harder inside of me, but slower now, slowing, slowing, drawing the orgasm out of me for as long as I can possibly take it, her thumb never lessening against my clit until the very last moment of pleasure that I'm capable of experiencing. Then, and only then, does she stop her motions; then and only then does she ease her fingers out of me, curling her hand around my thigh as I slump against her, still shuddering a little, bliss rolling through me so much that I lie my head on her shoulder and just breathe, wrapping my arms loosely around her as she curls her arms around me, too.

And I'm held gently, closely, by my angel.

For a long moment, I sit there, my eyes closed, just breathing against her, feeling her skin against me, body to body, heart to heart.

And then the want rises in me again.

I begin by kissing her shoulder. I press my mouth against her there, and then I trace my fingertips down both her shoulders so that she shivers against me. I trace my fingertips over her shoulder blades now, where I've seen her wings appear.

"Can I see them?" I whisper.

Gabrielle hesitates for only a heartbeat. She locks her gaze on mine, her burning turquoise gaze... And then, it happens.

They rise out of her shoulders, unfurling, feathers, feathers everywhere as Gabrielle lets her wings come out. Her wings, both shining, beautiful things, seem to arch over us, pressing against the cabinets above my head as they curl around us, shielding us from everything in the kitchen with their wall of shining white.

I reach up and slowly stroke one long feather, tracing my fingers up and up until I bury my hands into the softness of the feathers and, eventually, find the wing muscle beneath it. Gabrielle shudders against me as I brush my thumb against the wing itself, gently, softly. Her breathing is increasing again, and when Gabrielle looks at me, really looks at me, her turquoise eyes are darkened with such an absolute desire that another wave of the orgasm seems to roll through me in that moment.

It's now that I say, "Can we go to the

bedroom?" — not because the kitchen would be silly to have sex in; we just did it here, after all — but because I want the bed. I want the softness beneath her to cradle her wings, because I want her wings around us this time. I want her wings to surround us, shelter us, hold us, as I touch her.

So she nods only once, and she gently lifts me off the counter. My legs are still wrapped tightly around her, and I'm kissing her. I'm not getting down, not yet, and she doesn't want me to, as she grips my thighs tightly, and then she's walking to the bedroom as I hold onto her, as she carries me, my arms wrapped around her shoulders, my legs wrapped around her hips, the both of us kissing deeply.

Finally, we're in the bedroom, and she's pressing me down on the bed, and I let her, but when she arches over me again, I glance up at her mischievously, patting the bed beside me.

"You," I whisper, desire crackling over my skin, in every syllable of my words. "Here," I say softly, in a growl as I glance up at her, as I hold that gaze, desire in every atom of my being. "*Now.*"

And Gabrielle lifts one perfect brow, her mouth turning up at the corners, but she obeys, lying down on the bed beside me, curling her body toward me, one wing beneath her, folded seamlessly, the other curving above the both of us like some sort of bower, or a canopy bed of perfect, glowing feathers.

"As you wish," she whispers, turning to me, pressing her warm lips against my shoulder, opening her mouth, tracing her tongue against my skin.

Her wings curl up around us now as I get up, as I slide my right leg over hers, straddling her hips as she turns, lying on her back. She's still wearing the pinstripe pants, but I press my center down against her hips, just like I was doing out in the kitchen, and her breathing increases as she curls her fingers over my hips, hooking her fingers into the band of my panties.

"I don't want anything between us," she whispers then, her voice low, growling. I lean down, and I kiss her strongly. Fiercely.

"Nothing is," is what I tell her then, as I drag my panties off one leg, and then the other. I slide off of her, and then I'm undoing the clasp of her pants, tugging down at the zipper. I slide the pants off of her bottom, off of her entirely, dragging her panties—her silky, dark blue panties—off of her legs, too, tossing them in a heap on top of the pants on the floor.

She's beautiful. She's the most beautiful thing I've ever seen, with her wings curling up and around the both of us, holding us in a soft, white sphere of feathers and light, as I gently trace my fingers down her legs, urging them apart gently, gently, everything gentle. And Gabrielle complies, her legs falling open as I crawl between them.

I want to say a million things right now. I want to tell her that I love her, that I've been waiting my entire life for her. I want to tell her that every moment of my life has been leading up to this one—I just never knew it. Every moment leading me closer and closer to an angel.

But I find that I can't say anything at all. I'm speechless above her, her beauty too much, the connection between us too powerful for me to speak. And it's just as well. Words aren't needed. There are other languages.

So I use my mouth. I kiss her skin, I kiss her breasts, I kiss her center, trailing my tongue down and into her, and tasting heaven. I use my fingers, tracing patterns over her skin, her breasts, tracing patterns inside of the angel as she arches against me, crying out my name over and over again like it is her only prayer. Every inch of my body is used in this dance, as I touch her wings, as I touch her skin, the place over her heart, every atom of her, learning every line and curve of her, as she buries her fingers in my hair, as she curls and uncurls her toes, and I learn what makes her feel good, what makes her feel *very* good, and as I lick her clit, what makes her feel orgasmic. There's a brief, bright shudder of her against me as I lick, over and over again, tasting the deliciousness of all that is Gabrielle, and then she's coming against me, the angel shuddering against me, her wings shuddering around us until they fall heavily beside her on the bed because she's no longer capable of holding them up.

I rise over her then, straddling her hips, trailing kisses up her belly, kissing her belly button as I smile against her, and then I'm kissing each of her breasts, lingering on them as she sighs beneath me, tracing her fingers over my own shoulders. Finally, I kiss along her neck, and then I capture her mouth as she buries her hands in my hair, pulling me down on top of her.

We kiss for a long, perfect moment, the length of our bodies pressed close to one another. She wraps her arms around me tightly, holding me to her, and finally I fall into the crook of her arm as one of her wings tiredly folds across the both of us like a blanket. It's so soft as it curls around the two of us that I shiver against her a little.

"Well," is what Gabrielle says then, and it sounds like a marvel, that word. *Well.* She breathes it out with as much reverence as she spoke my name earlier, and I smile against her skin, stroking the wingtip that curls over my cheek. "Well," she repeats, her words soft as she turns her head, pressing a kiss against the top of mine. "I did it," she whispers against me.

I laugh a little, looking up at her. "Did what?"

Gabrielle laughs, too, peals of weak laughter that fill the bedroom, and I'm staring at her, chuckling a little as I wrap an arm around her shoulders.

"Okay, okay," she says, wiping a tear from the corner of her eye as she shakes her head, still laughing. "So, we Seraphim have a saying," she tells me, with another shake of her head. "It's not a particularly clever saying. It's not even original. I think we stole it from you mortals, actually. Ready to hear it?"

I nod, mystified, as I smile at her.

"*Carpe pisces,*" Gabrielle whispers then, her tone still utterly reverent.

I stare at her then, utterly perplexed. "Wait. It's...seize the...fish?"

"Well, like I said, it isn't clever, but it makes sense, doesn't it?" asks Gabrielle sincerely, holding me close.

I'm laughing now against her, my shoulders shaking. "No," I chuckle. "It doesn't make any sense at all."

Gabrielle snorts, then rolls over a little so that she's on top of me again, her wings flexing and curling around her shoulders now. "Think about it," says Gabrielle, her head to the side as she leans down, bending her head to me. She's straddling me, and her wet center is against my hips, and she instantly has my attention. I'm realizing that this first round was just that...a first round. And there are going to be others very, very shortly.

I thought my body was utterly spent at this point, but I was wrong. Turns out, I'm just getting started.

"If you're a bear," Gabrielle whispers mischievously, placing a kiss on my collarbone, "and you're trying to catch a fish for your dinner, you can't dilly-dally and worry about whether or not the fish you catch will be a nice, juicy one or one of those dry, bland ones. Or whether it will bite you. You just have to grab it. Seize the fish! Live in the moment, because moments — or...fish — are all that matters."

I sit up on my elbows, and I capture Gabrielle's mouth with a kiss. "I hope you know," I tell her, kissing her again, "that that's adorable. *You're* adorable."

I'm completely surprised, because for the very first time since I've known Gabrielle, her cheeks are actually reddening. Gabrielle is *blushing*.

"And you know what?" she says then, her smile softening. "I *did* it. I seized the fish. Because you taught me something."

I watch her arching over me, breathless. "What could I have possibly taught an angel?" I whisper to her.

Gabrielle pauses then, pauses with her palms flat against my stomach, pauses with her wings shielding us from the outside world, so that it's just Gabrielle and me and nothing else besides.

"I was afraid of falling," Gabrielle whispers then, her words feather soft. "But I really didn't have anything to fear. Not really." She bends low, then, her mouth an inch from my own as she holds my gaze. "Fear," she whispers, her eyes bright, "is always imaginary. And only love is real."

Inside of me, my heart soars as high as an angel as Gabrielle wraps her wings around the both of us, and we kiss again.

And we keep kissing.

Chapter 7: The Reason for Wings

"Well, *someone's* in a good mood."

I toss the packet of M&M's at Scott's head but miss because he catches them in midair.

"Seriously, let's make a list. You're *whistling* like you're a frickin' *cartoon* character or something," says Scott, ticking off his fingers with one brow raised. "You didn't make faces at me during the weekly meeting this morning, despite the big 'go get 'em' speech that Brian gave us, and you *always* make faces. And you *willingly* said you'd cover the National Clam Chowder Awards. I mean, I feel like I don't even know you anymore," he teases me, breaking open the M&M's packet.

I hold out my hand as he picks out all of the brown M&M's and puts them in my palm. "You're the weirdo who won't eat brown M&M's, and you're calling *my* cheerful mood weird?" I ask him, crunching happily on the chocolate. "These are so good."

"See?" he shouts triumphantly, pointing at me as he munches on his own M&M's. Bits of chocolate shoot out of his mouth, but he keeps talking. "You always say that M&M's taste cheap, that you don't even *like* them. Which, by the way, *who doesn't like M&Ms*? But c'mon, spill. Something's up. Is it about that woman you introduced me to? Your new *girlfriend*?" Scott says the word "girlfriend" like an annoying younger brother might, and I'm laughing as he beams at me.

"Yes," I tell him with a happy sigh as I slump back into my office chair. "It *is* because of my girlfriend. Scott, I'm totally in love," I say, spreading my hands.

He slaps me five, then takes another handful of M&M's and shoves them into his mouth as I feel a caress of feathers against my cheek; I shiver.

I already had to make Gabrielle swear (on whatever angels swear on) that she wouldn't do anything...well...*sexy* to me while she was invisible today. "I have a job to do," I'd warned her, as she tickled the back of my neck with her right wing while I was putting on my makeup this morning. "No shenanigans," I said, shaking my mascara at her.

"Angel's honor," she'd promised, her face perfectly serious, before she pressed my front against the bathroom counter and sneaked her fingers under the edge of my skirt.

"You're blushing!" says Scott now, staring at me with a huge smile. "Oh, my God, so what *happened* this weekend?"

"Oh, you know. It was just...a good

weekend," I tell him, biting my lip as my blush intensifies. I glance up at the clock. Two minutes until I'm out of here. "Anyway," I tell him, grabbing my purse from under the desk, "I'm introducing her to Ginger tonight for the first time, which is *super* exciting."

"Seriously!" says Scott, both of his eyebrows up now. "You *never* introduce your girlfriends to Ginger. What gives?"

I stare at him, blinking. "That's not true..." I start, but then I think about it, and I realize that it *is* true. I don't usually make a habit of introducing *any* of my girlfriends to Ginger. She's probably met only three or four of them over the years, and that's, well, weird.

But I know why I do it. I don't want Ginger to meet women who I'm not going to stay with. A woman who isn't *the one*.

Ginger is my best friend. She's been with me through thick and thin. In the back of my head, I've always known that it's important, introducing the best friend to the girlfriend, and I've always been a pretty casual dater, so it never came up often...

Until Gabrielle. Until my guardian angel.

So tonight's the night. Tonight's the night that Gabrielle becomes really *real* in my life. Because Gabrielle and Ginger are going to meet face to face.

And I couldn't be more thrilled.

"So, where are you gals going to dinner?"

asks Scott, his ears perked up. He's such a foodie. I chuckle as I toss my cell phone into my purse.

"The Boston Tea Party," I tell him with a wink. He rolls his eyes. It's a popular tourist destination, but locals still go there and enjoy it, too. The only real reason that I wanted to meet Ginger there was that I thought Gabrielle would get a kick out of the restaurant's decor.

"Far be it from me to judge your culinary choices," chuckles Scott, holding up his hands as I stand. "Hey, have a seriously great time, okay?" he tells me with a happy grin. "I'm thrilled for you, Erin. I'm so glad you're happy."

"I hope you're still happy for me tomorrow when we cover that Clam Chowder Awards ceremony that I signed us up for," I tease him, as I sling my purse over my shoulder.

"Hey, it's no monkey, but it pays the bills," says Scott, waving me out.

I practically race out of the news building and down onto the sidewalk where Gabrielle is now leaning against the concrete stair railing, her hands buried deep in her pockets and her face lighting up like the sun when she sees me. It's her face, that pure, incandescent joy when she catches a glimpse of me, that remakes me from the inside out, and then I'm running up to her, wrapping my arms around her neck as she lifts me up a little, spinning me around and crushing my body to hers so that she can kiss me close.

"Let's go," she tells me then, and kissing me once more for good measure (she's so hot and soft and tastes like cinnamon, and I really don't want to stop kissing her), she takes my arm and tucks it through hers snugly, and we begin to stroll down the sidewalk together.

"So, The Boston Tea Party is a pub," I tell her with a smile. "It serves classic Boston fare, and the decorations are pretty cool. I think you're going to love it."

"I'm a little nervous," says Gabrielle softly, surprising no one more than me. I blink at her.

"Because of meeting Ginger?" I ask her. "Don't worry," I tell her then, patting her arm, "she's going to love you. I mean, she can be a little forward, but that's just Ginger—"

"It's not that," says Gabrielle, wrinkling her nose. She sighs, shaking her head a little. "I mean...you're going out on a limb introducing me to someone you care so much about," she says, holding my gaze. "What if..." She trails off with another sigh.

Every moment, this lingers between us unspoken: *What if my mission ends, and I have to leave?* she's thinking. I know, because I'm thinking it, too.

All weekend long, we danced around the possibility. It sneaked between us and would appear when I least expected it. When we ate ice cream together, naked on the couch (laughing when the melted ice cream dripped onto my chest, and then gasping in delight as Gabrielle licked it off), when we took Sawyer for a walk to get hot dogs, when we watched a new, terrible Lifetime movie. And, yes, even though the weekend was beautiful, perfect, really, the possibility of all of this ending abruptly, far too soon, was there. Constant, omnipresent.

And terribly chilling.

We've just started this, this "us." And to think that it could be snatched away so quickly...

But I tell Gabrielle now what I told myself all weekend, every time I would think about it:

"Hey, *carpe pisces*, all right?" I squeeze her arm. I smile softly up at her and am gratified by a returned smile, her beautiful mouth curving at the corners. "Right now," I tell my angel, holding her arm close to me, "you're not disappearing, right? You're right here, and we're together, and that's a wonderful thing. Right now, right this moment..." I take a deep breath. "You're here. I'm here. We're alive, and we're together." My heart squeezes inside of me as I hold tightly to her hand. "The most important thing in the world to me, right now, is us," I tell her, my voice lowering as I hold her gaze. "I'm so happy you're here with me." My voice catches, emotions making the words come out thickly. I clear my throat, blink away the tears that are threatening to be shed.

"Me, too, Erin," Gabrielle tells me then, her voice catching. "Me, too," she repeats, and then she stops walking—we both do—and right in the middle of the sidewalk, she steps close to me, curls her fingers into my hair and around the back of my neck, her skin hot and soft against my own, and she kisses me. It's a lingering kiss, this one, done with a subtle grace that I have learned to adore in my angel.

There's something poignant about this moment, something that makes my heart ache, and deeply...but I shove that feeling away. *No*, I tell myself, drinking her deep. *Stay in the moment. Right now is all that matters. Right here. Right now.*

But as she kisses me so tenderly, as I kiss her back, something twists in my gut, deep inside.

It's a bad feeling.

I push it away, just as much as I hold her close, and then Gabrielle presses her forehead against mine. "Ready?" she asks me with a soft smile.

"Yeah," I tell her, the butterflies churning in my stomach as I try to ignore them. Together, hand in hand, we make our way down the rest of the block and into The Boston Tea Party.

It's this great little pub that, no matter what Scott says, is a really fun place. Scott's a foodie—if he's not eating at a gastronomy bar, or whatever they're called these days, he thinks the food is sub par. But how can anyone *not* like a great veggie burger and fries? Obviously, the pub itself is Boston Tea Party-themed, which means that when you step inside, it's like you've just descended into the belly of a ship, complete with wooden ship hull walls and beams overhead, with old farm lanterns hanging down. The tables in the booths along the walls are made of overturned wooden tea crates, and they have about twenty different kinds of tea on the menu here, just to complete the "tea party" ambiance. The waiters and waitresses all wear old colonial garb, and you're given a tea bag that you can throw into their ocean-themed fountain in the center of the restaurant, to feel like you've made yourself part of the historical festivities.

It's pure kitsch, through and through, but the food is good (they seriously have a kick-ass veggie burger), and—just as I thought—the minute we get inside, Gabrielle is enthralled by everything.

But she's not excited for the reasons I thought she'd be...

"They've got it all wrong," is what Gabrielle says when the waiter sees us to our table and asks us if we'd like our tea bags to throw into the fountain *now* or after dinner. "This isn't how the Boston Tea Party *actually* went," Gabrielle begins to the waiter, but I tell him that we need a minute with the menu, and then she falls silent with a huge, apologetic smile.

"Sorry," she says, biting her lip. "It's just that I *was* there, and it really didn't involve *tea* in *bags*..." She trails off, shaking her head with a little chuckle. "It was a pretty interesting night, actually, that Boston Tea Party," she tells me wryly.

"See...there's so much I want to talk to you about," I finally say, reaching across the table and taking her hand. "You know?" I search her face. "You've been through *so much*. I mean, you're an *angel*, for heaven's sake. You were probably there for the beginning of the universe—"

"Surprisingly, it wasn't that much to look at," she says with a grin.

I stare at her. "But...but see?" I splutter. "You were *there*. And I want to know *everything*. Like...what happens when we die? And where did we come from? Where are we going?" I fall silent for a minute, holding her gaze. "Is there really someone out there who cares enough about us to send us angels?" I ask her quietly.

Gabrielle smiles at me then, and her smile is so warm and bright and comforting that I'm filled with calm from the inside out: calm, and this overwhelming love that makes me feel like my heart is growing inside of me.

"Erin," she whispers, taking my hand across the table, threading her fingers through mine and squeezing gently, her palm warm against my skin. "If you knew every bit of the wonder in the universe, if you saw every star being born, and every galaxy blossoming right in front of your nose, you would still know what you know now." She lifts her chin, her turquoise eyes sparkling. "And that is," she whispers, lifting my hand from the table, bringing it close to her lips, "that love is the only power. And love is all that's real." She brings my knuckles to her mouth, and she kisses me gently, her warmth radiating through me.

My heartbeat thunders, fast and frenzied, as I stare at this woman I adore utterly, this woman I'm falling head over heels in love with. So I tell her the truest thing I know:

"I love you," I whisper to her, and she flicks her glittering turquoise gaze to me, her eyes wide. She looks like she's going to say something, too...

And then the front door of the restaurant opens.

It's been opening and shutting multiple times while we've been sitting at this table—the table closest to the door. But, just then, it opens and stays open, and people begin to pour in, a crowd moving into the pub.

I normally wouldn't notice this, but it seems that every single person—male and female alike—are dressed like they're about to go to a wedding. Or a funeral. The men are all wearing suits, as are some of the women, and the rest of the women are wearing very formal dresses.

And most of the people have shaded their eyes with dark glasses. And they have...guns?

Wait, what?

"Um..." I mutter, sitting bolt upright and paying attention.

And then, in through the front door—impossibly—walks the President of the United States.

I blink a couple of times for good measure, because, for a long moment, I can't be certain that what I'm seeing is real. I mean, President Patterson, *really*? But, yes—it's totally her. As a news reporter, her image is, of course, emblazoned on my mind. And since she's our country's very first female president, she's probably the most recognizable President the country has ever had.

President Amanda Patterson is very short in person, only reaching up to my shoulders. She's wearing a bright red suit with a knee-length skirt, and her shoulder-length black hair is perfectly styled into a bun at the top of her head. She smiles at everyone in the pub, offering little waves, and then someone else steps forward. I've seen him on some of the broadcasts Patterson has given the country. He's like her right-hand guy.

"Please, everyone continue to enjoy your dinner," he says, smiling as his booming voice carries through the restaurant. "Air Force One was experiencing a little technical trouble, so we had to land at Logan, and President Patterson, of course, wanted to come sample some of her favorite dishes from The Boston Tea Party."

A cheer goes up in the pub, because—of course—we're big fans of Patterson here. Patterson was originally from Boston, and that she stopped *here* of all places means really good things for the pub itself. The place is probably going to have a line going around the building for months now, because everyone's going to remember the time that President Patterson came for dinner.

I'm grabbing my phone out of my purse before even more of the secret servicemen can make it into the building, and I have it pressed to my ear instantly. I wait semi-patiently for the ringing to stop and for Scott to pick up.

Gabrielle grins at me, one of her brows raised, and I smile hugely back at her.

"Scott!" I whisper into the phone when he answers with, "Hello? Erin?"

"Scott, listen, I'm sitting in The Boston Tea Party, and the *President* just walked in. Like, President Patterson," I tell him in one big rush of breath. "Can you look up some details for me *right now* and then get over here *right now*?"

"I'm still at the station. I can be there in a minute if you think I can get in," he says, sounding as excited as a five-year-old at

Christmas. "I'd heard she was in town. Apparently, according to the Associated Press wires," he says distractedly, trying to pick up his camera, look something up online and talk to me, all at once, "the President had to make an unexpected stop. She was traveling to her private retreat in Maine when her jet had mechanical issues just as they were nearing Boston. So she thought she'd pay a quick visit to her home turf. Look, Erin, I'll be right there, okay, because *no one* has this scoop yet. Oh, my God, do you think this is it? Our breakout story?"

"I think so, but get your butt over here!" I whisper to him; then I'm hanging up and staring at Gabrielle across the table from me. I reach over and hold tightly to her hands. "This could really be our big chance! At last!" I whisper to her, thrills racing over my skin and making me shiver a little as my blood pounds through my veins. This impossible, awesome opportunity has just happened to me, and I'm going to make the most of it.

Gabrielle and I turn in our seats, and we both watch as the President makes her way through the restaurant. President Patterson has a regal grace about her, and she's kind to every single person she speaks to. She stops at a few tables, smiles and shakes the hands of the people sitting there, the people who are experiencing just as much excitement as I feel. "It's so nice to meet you, Ms. President," says one guy, practically spluttering with happiness as he pumps Patterson's hand up and down.

Beyond Patterson, I can see the door of the restaurant open again. It's getting pretty crowded in here, and the secret servicemen and women are gathered tightly at the entrance. But still, Ginger manages to squeeze on through, muttering about how she has an appointment, and she better *damn* well be allowed in a public restaurant, thankyouverymuch, as she elbows her way past the secret servicemen and into the restaurant itself. Ginger could probably make her way into anyplace in the world, and she uses her powers now to shoulder into The Boston Tea Party.

I make an "over here!" motion with my hands, waving, and Ginger spots me. With a wide grin, she starts to make a beeline toward our table.

"What the heck?" she asks, glancing around when she finally reaches me. Ginger is still dressed from work and is wearing a tailored suit, but you can tell that she drove her Jeep here with the top down, because her hair is crazy, pointed in every direction. Ginger glances around, taking off her sunglasses with wide eyes. "Is, like, Madonna here or something? Why are there so many guns and sunglasses?" she quips. She reaches out and hauls me toward her for a tight hug.

"Not Madonna," I tell her with a huge smile. "*Better* than Madonna."

And then I point over my shoulder.

"It's just the President of the United States," I tell her quietly, inclining my head behind me toward the President.

I don't think I've ever seen Ginger speechless in her life; she *always* has something to say. But she's speechless now. Her jaw falls open, and she glances over my shoulder at President Patterson, who has made her way up to one of the payment booths and is ordering fries to go from a starstruck waiter in a tri-corner hat.

"It's the President of the United States," whispers Ginger almost reverently. "And she's *here*. Where we're having our *dinner*. *President Patterson* came to The Boston Tea Party! I mean, is this awesome, or is this awesome?" she asks, practically bouncing in place. I'm *fairly* certain that the only other time I've seen her this happy was the time she caught the Red Sox foul ball.

"Scott's coming here with the camera because this is the story of a *lifetime*," I tell her hurriedly, "but I'm going to take a little home video with my cell phone camera, just in case he doesn't get here in time." And then I blink, realizing I've forgotten to do something *very* important. I turn, putting an arm around Gabrielle's waist as she grins at me, patiently waiting for an introduction. "Oh, wait, wait,

243

President or no President...Ginger, this is Gabrielle," I tell Ginger, beaming with pride as I squeeze Gabrielle's waist. "And Gabrielle, this is Ginger," I tell her, smiling at my best friend.

My angel holds out her hand to Ginger, and they shake warmly, smiling at one another.

"I'm so excited to finally meet you," says Gabrielle enthusiastically. "I've heard so much about you, and I know how important you are to Erin."

"Likewise," says Ginger, her smile growing even bigger. "You're right, Erin," she tells me then with a wink. "She's pretty hot."

"I'm going to punch your arm later," I tell her with a raised brow as I lift up my cell phone and press *record* on the camera function. "Crap, the lighting in here is terrible," I mutter. "I'll be right back, okay? I want to see if I can get some better video quality." I inch out of the booth and walk a little to the right, trying to angle myself under one of the farm lanterns.

"I wonder if there's a line for the bathroom?" I hear Ginger ask, and Gabrielle points toward the restrooms—no line at all. Ginger slides out of the booth.

And just like that moment when the car almost hit me, it seems like everything in the world slows...down...

My bad feeling never went away, but for some reason now, no reason that I can make out, it intensifies, my intuition telling me that something *very* close by is about to go very, very wrong.

I turn my head, watching the President ordering her fries as Ginger moves past me, aiming for the bathroom. Ginger's not close to the President, not by a long shot; she's about twenty feet away from Patterson, but she's crossing in front of the President in my line of vision.

I whirl around, my heart thundering in my chest.

By now, most of the people in the restaurant are standing, craning to get a better view, and there are more people coming through the front door all the time, because word is getting out now, and the people of Boston want to see their President. It's understandable, but the room is starting to fill up to capacity, the manager of The Boston Tea Party trying to wade through all of the people so that he can get to the front door and close it against further entrants. But he's not making much progress. Instead, the people are starting to move toward the President, crowding her, and the manager is caught up with them.

And so is Ginger. She's starting to be pushed toward the President because of the crowd of onlookers.

Gabrielle, directly behind me, calls out my name. I turn and try to look at her; she looks wide-eyed, stiff. And then she says, "No—"

And I realize that one of the secret servicemen in front of me has pulled out a gun.

I'm so confused. Yeah, there are a bunch of people in here, and they're all pressed together pretty tightly, but there's no one doing anything but talking happily. I look around the restaurant to see who might be threatening the President, looking very closely, but I see nothing.

And that's when the secret serviceman lowers the gun and points it at the President.

And, because of where Ginger is now, swept along with the crowd and being pushed toward the President...the secret serviceman is pointing that gun directly at Ginger.

I don't even think. I'm shouting, but my voice is swallowed in the cacophony of the crowd all around me. I move, then, moving as quickly as I can, and since time seems to have slowed down, everything is clearer, brighter, but I'm not fast enough. I can never be fast enough, I realize, as my heart rises in my throat. I'm walking through quicksand, but it doesn't matter. A secret serviceman is pointing a gun at Ginger, and I don't know why, but it can't be for anything good. All I know is that *I have to reach her*.

And I do. I finally reach Ginger, and I'm throwing myself at her, pointing to the secret serviceman. "He has a gun!" I yell into Ginger's ear, and she stares at me as if I just told her Santa

Claus is real, but then she's staring along the line of sight from my pointed finger, and she sees that, yes, a secret serviceman has a gun, and, yes, he's pointing it at her. She takes one step backward, eyes wide, and then I'm shouting again, though I don't quite get the words out, because suddenly a lot of things happen all at once.

There's a gunshot.

In this relatively small, crowded space, among so many people, the gunshot sounds like an explosion, an explosion so loud that I feel the sound deep in my bones. Instantly, I turn, my body turns, but it's so slow, and I'm moving entirely on instinct. Because the bullet is aimed for Ginger, and I'm not going to let *that* happen. I step forward, stepping into the bullet's trajectory, the sound of the gunshot jarring my body like a violent impact...

But then I *do* feel an impact, because I'm crashing to the floor...but it's not because the bullet hit me.

It's because Gabrielle just slammed into me.

I saw her, moving through the air. I saw the glint of wings, the shimmery light of the white feathers...and then she hit me hard, and I crumpled to the ground, my angel heavy on top of me.

For a long moment, I can't hear, and I can hardly see. There's panic; people are running everywhere, and as I blink slowly, I can see feet rushing past my head. I must have hit my head, because there's a hazy, white glow around everything. I shake my head a little, pressing my fingers to my temple. Then I take my hand away and stare down at it, because there's a little blood on my fingertips. But as I stare down at that blood, I *know* that it's not my blood. I sit up, and then my hearing comes back with such a loud rush, it's like a punch to the gut. There's screaming. And Ginger is kneeling on the ground next to an unmoving body.

For half of a heartbeat, before I take in the entirety of the scene, I think, in the farthest reaches of my brain, that it's the President of the United States that Ginger is leaning over on the floor, her eyes wide, her mouth in an O of shock. But it's not the President of the United States on the floor.

It's the body of Gabrielle.

There are people shouting for an ambulance. In the background, I'm aware of the fact that the secret serviceman with the gun, who obviously fired that shot, is being disarmed and pummeled to the ground, but it's all happening in a space that doesn't really matter to me. Nothing matters to me at all as I crawl over to Gabrielle's side, my head shaking back and forth, back and forth in disbelief, as a sob ricochets through me, a low moan escaping my mouth.

"Gabrielle?" I whisper, reaching out and brushing my fingertips over the lapel of her pinstripe suit jacket. The jacket that's soaked through with blood in the shoulder, blood that is *so red* against the white and black of her suit.

The fabric is becoming saturated as blood leaks up and out of the bullet wound right over Gabrielle's heart.

"No," I whisper, because I press my fingers to her neck now, feeling for a pulse. I wondered if angels have hearts, have blood, have a pulse, but I know she has a pulse—I felt her pulse this weekend, over and over again, as I kissed every inch of her skin. I felt the flutter of her heartbeat beneath my mouth as I pressed a kiss to the hollow of her throat, to her eyelids, to her lips. But there's no pulse there now, in every place I kissed... There's no pulse at all. Her eyes are closed. And she's not breathing.

"You can't be," I whisper, sinking back onto my heels and staring down at my angel. That's exactly it. *She's an angel.* This isn't supposed to happen. She can't be killed! She's supposed to save my life and disappear, go back home, and I'll never see her again, but that would be better than this. Because she's still here. She's lying on the ground without a pulse, without a breath.

She's gone.

I pick up Gabrielle's hand, the hand that buried itself in my hair, the hand that brushed fingertips over my body, the hand that held my hand so many times, and I lift her palm to my mouth, pressing a kiss there as a sob wracks my body. "Please don't go," I whisper, and I repeat it, over and over again. "Please don't go. Please stay with me," I tell her, sobbing brokenly. "I need you...please. Please don't go, Gabrielle. I love you."

Nothing happens. Gabrielle remains silent on the floor as the secret servicemen and women make a wide circle around us, pressing the people back, and Ginger puts an arm around my shoulders, telling me that it's going to be okay.

"This wasn't supposed to happen," I tell Ginger, weeping, tears streaking down my face, my breath coming in tiny bursts. "No, you don't understand," I tell her, when she makes another soothing noise. I glance up at my best friend with wild eyes. "She's an *angel*. She's not supposed to die," I tell Ginger, who stares at me now, but in that pained expression of thinking I've gone off the deep end and not exactly wanting to tell me. But I don't care. It's the truth, and I've finally told Ginger the truth. And it's too late.

"She's not supposed to *die*," I repeat, pressing Gabrielle's hand to my mouth, kissing her skin, closing my eyes, rage and frustration and a deep, abiding ache ricocheting through my body.

And then the hand against my mouth...moves.

I start, immediately staring down at Gabrielle, desperate for *any* sign of life, but then I get a whole bunch of them as my angel opens her eyes, inhaling a deep breath, her mouth parted as she inhales. Then she blinks, once or twice, and glances up at me, her brows furrowed. "I'm...still here?" she whispers, her voice low and gravelly, like she hasn't spoken in a year. But it's still the most beautiful voice I've ever heard.

I cry with relief and fall forward onto Gabrielle, peppering her face with kisses as Gabrielle glances up at me with a weak smile, brushing her fingers across my face, the pad of her thumb wiping away my tears. She then gazes thoughtfully down at the blood that's soaked through the hole in her jacket from the wound on her chest. But Gabrielle unbuttons her shirt slowly, peeling the fabric to reveal...no wound at all. There's blood, pooling on the surface of unmarred skin, like she was never wounded, as if—instead—someone spilled movie paint on her.

"Well, that doesn't happen every day," says Gabrielle then, and I squeeze her so tightly, half-laughing, half-crying that she makes a little squeak and pats my shoulder. "Gentle, my love," she says softly in my ear. And then: "Something...happened," Gabrielle tells me weakly, reaching up and cupping my face with her hands.

"You were shot," I whisper to her, happy tears streaming down my face. "You...you took a *bullet* for me."

"No. I mean, yes, yes, I did," she tells me, her smile growing. "But I mean...while I was asleep just now. Something happened. I went somewhere."

"What?" I whisper down at her, confused. "You're here, Gabrielle," I tell her, wrapping my arms around her and holding her close. "You stayed with me," I whisper into her ear, joy and elation soaring through me, chasing away the adrenaline of fear.

"Erin," says Gabrielle, pulling me so that I'm staring down at her now, nose to nose. "Before anything else happens...I love you."

I stare at her, love making my heart expand inside of me, and then Gabrielle is kissing me, her mouth warm and soft as a feather, and my angel is *alive,* and she's *kissing me.* I don't think I've ever felt happier than I do, right here, right in this moment.

A cheer erupts in the restaurant, and then shouts of, "She's alive!" begin to ripple through the crowd.

"Listen to me," says Gabrielle softly, staring deeply into my eyes with her own unwavering gaze. "Normally... Normally on a mission, I'd save you, and that'd be it. I'd just...disappear and go home. But that's not what happened here," she tells me, all in a rush. "Instead, I was taken somewhere, and I was given a choice."

I shake my head, confused. "What do you—"

"I was offered the choice to stay. Here. With you. That is, apparently," she tells me with a soft smile, "what *falling* is."

I stare at her, my eyes growing wider, my heartbeat surging through me. "What did you choose?" I manage to whisper.

Gabrielle smiles, a smile so bright it mirrors the sun. "Remember that time I told you there was nowhere else I'd rather be than by your side?"

I'm crying again, happy tears streaming down my face. "Yes," I manage.

"Well," she whispers, holding my gaze, her eyes twinkling, "an angel never tells a lie."

I lean down, and I capture her mouth with my own. I kiss her, and then I have to wipe away the happy tears as I splutter: "So you're staying? You're, what, mortal now?"

Gabrielle pauses, considers, shakes her head. "I don't know. Maybe. I suppose I must be." Her smile turns wry. "Best not to risk another bullet through the heart to test out that theory."

"No," I agree. "Never again. Thank you," I whisper, staring down at her, "for saving my life."

"It was my greatest pleasure," Gabrielle whispers, lifting my hand to her mouth and kissing the back of it, never taking her gaze from me.

"Whoa, what just happened?" Scott is suddenly there, his sneakers by Gabrielle's head as he stares down at us, his camera cocked on his shoulder. "Are you okay, Gabrielle? What just happened?" He's spluttering as he looks from me to Ginger to Gabrielle, and back to me again. I don't ask Scott how he got past the heightened security. I'm kind of wondering, with this secret serviceman having pulled a gun on the President, how much of those "mechanical troubles" on the plane were actually a setup, and how much of the secret servicemen were in on trying to take the President down. Either way, the entire restaurant is in chaos, so maybe Scott wiggled through pretty easily.

"It's a long story, Scottie," says Gabrielle, summing up the evening well as she sits up on her elbows and smiles at me.

The President of the United States presses through the crowd then. "I want to talk to the woman who saved my life," she's saying severely to a secret serviceman. I guess Gabrielle saved her life, too, as much as mine. And Ginger's. Gabrielle saved *several* people's lives tonight. I'm staring up at the President, and then Gabrielle takes hold of my hand again.

"Seize the fish," she whispers, and I nod, standing.

"Hello, Ms. President," I tell Patterson, holding out my hand to the President of the United States. She takes it and shakes it firmly, smiling. "I'd like to introduce you to my girlfriend, Gabrielle," I tell her, as Scott turns his camera on, and I help Gabrielle up from the ground.

"Gabrielle!" says Patterson, and holds out her hand. "Thank you for saving my life," she tells my angel.

"Don't mention it," Gabrielle quips as she snakes an arm around my waist. "It was all in the line of duty," she tells the President modestly.

"Well, I certainly appreciate it!" says President Patterson. "Can I buy you ladies some fries?"

"I think we'd like that," says Gabrielle, beaming down on me.

And President Patterson buys us fries, veggie burgers and Cokes as I ask her questions about foreign policy and her favorite childhood books, Gabrielle beside me for every minute of it.

And what could have become the day I died instead becomes the best and *weirdest* day of my life.

"Do you want to take your silver blouse?" asks Gabrielle, holding it up in front of her. "The shimmery one? It's quite pretty," she says, eyeing me with her narrowed, sultry gaze, the one she reserves for undressing me with her eyes. And she's not exactly looking at my face when she says this. I'm laughing as I take the blouse from her.

"I'm taking practically everything I own at this point, and I can only check one bag," I tell her gently, before straddling her lap. She's sitting on the edge of the bed, but I push her down easily, because she *wants* to be pushed down, back onto our bed.

And then I'm kissing her.

It's been a few months since Gabrielle saved my life...in more ways than one. A few months since the bullet that was going to pierce me through—because I was in the wrong place at the wrong time—propelled itself into Gabrielle's shoulder, instead. A few months since Gabrielle chose to stay with me instead of going home.

"Well, I think you *should* take everything you own," Gabrielle tells me, when I pin her wrists by her head and give her a mischievous smile. I begin to trail a pattern of kisses from her mouth down her neck. "After all, it's not every day that you get your first overseas story," she tells me, and I can hear the pride in her voice. "It's pretty spectacular, Erin. *You're* pretty spectacular."

"I wouldn't have gotten this story if I hadn't gotten the President story," I tell her gently, kissing her jaw. "And I wouldn't have gotten the President story if you hadn't saved my life, so—"

"Like I told you, it was my greatest pleasure," Gabrielle breathes, as I kiss the hollow of her throat. She tells me this at least once a day now, and I believe it. Because everything about her is *my* greatest pleasure.

We are inseparable. And we are madly in love. And this might never have happened, all of this. I know, without a shadow of a doubt, how lucky I am.

I stop kissing her for a moment, and I rise above her, looking down at my angel, who is—technically—my angel no longer. I trail my fingertips up her arms to her shoulders, lingering there as I frown a little. "Do you ever miss it?" I whisper, embracing her tightly, closing my eyes and remembering those beautiful wings.

"Miss what?" she whispers, brushing her warm lips against my forehead.

"Being, you know, *immortal*. An angel. Having wings... Flying."

Gabrielle kisses me deeply, then, cupping her hand around the back of my neck and drawing me to her like gravity. "Never," she whispers, holding my gaze. Her eyes aren't turquoise anymore, not really. Instead, they're a piercing human blue, so bright that they still take my breath away. "Not for one millisecond," she growls to me, shaking her head. "And you know why?"

"Why?" I whisper.

"Because," Gabrielle breathes, holding me close, "*you're* the reason I had wings, Erin. My whole life, from the beginning of time...I was always flying toward you."

"I love you," I tell her, kissing her fiercely. "I'm so glad you found me. That I found you."

She breathes slowly, almost reverently, as she returns the kiss. "I love you, too," says Gabrielle, former angel, now lifelong love, dog walker, grilled-cheese-toast burner and everything wonderful in between.

I don't claim to know how the universe works or how angels exist, or how my angel found me...but one thing is perfectly clear.

Love is the most powerful force in the universe.

"Now, do you want me to cook dinner?" asks Gabrielle mischievously, waggling her eyebrows at me.

"No!" I almost shout, before she pulls me onto the bed beside her, holding me close and laughing.

And love is all that's real.

The End

The Guardian Angel

If you enjoyed *The Guardian Angel*, you'll love Bridget's Sullivan Vampires.

The following is an excerpt from "**Eternal Hotel**," the first novella in the Sullivan Vampires series, a beautiful, romantic epic that follows the clan of Sullivan vampires and the women who love them. Advance praise has hailed this hallmark series as "*Twilight* for women who love women" and "a lesbian romance that takes vampires seriously! Two thumbs up!"

…So *this* was the staircase from last night, next to the front desk. The Widowmaker. It must be. I'd never seen a steeper set of stairs. From up above, they looked simply like the rungs of a ladder in a barn—so steep and so tall and almost impossible to even think of taking.

It's not that I don't like heights—I'm pretty okay with them. But these stairs were something else. I wasn't taking these steps—I'd have to circle back somehow and find the other spiral staircase down to the first floor

As I turned, I caught the first floor out of the corner of my eye. Because of the cathedral ceilings of that first floor, it seemed much farther away then I'd thought it was.

It was then that something strange happened.

The ground seemed to spin under me for a moment, bucking and heaving like I was trying to walk on waves of carpeting, not good firm floor. Or did it really? Was it just a trick of the eye? Either way, I took a step backward as a shadow fell in front of me, but there was no floor beneath that foot stepping backward, then, and I was *tumbling* backwards, shock cold enough to burn me flooding through my body as, impossibly, I began to fall down the stairs.

A hand caught my arm. I hung suspended over the abyss of the air, my back to the emptiness, and in one smooth motion, I was pulled back.

Saved.

The hand was cold, and the body I brushed against as I was hauled out of the air felt as if the person had stepped out of a prolonged trip through a walk-in freezer. I looked up at the face of the woman who had saved me, and when I breathed out, I will never forget it: my breath hung suspended in the air between us like a ghost.

She was taller than me by about a head, and I had to lean back to gaze into her eyes. They were violently blue, a blue that opened me up like a key and lock as she looked down at me, her eyes sharp and dark as her jaw worked, her full lips in a downward curve that my own eyes couldn't help but follow. She wore a ponytail, the cascades of her silken white-blonde hair gathered tightly at the back of her head and flowing over her right shoulder like frozen water falling. She wore a man's suit, I realized, complete with a navy blue tie smartly pulled snug against her creamy neck. She looked pale and felt so cold as her strong hand gripped my wrist, but it was gentle, too. As if she knew her own strength.

I saw all of this in an instant, my eyes following the lines and curves of her like I'd trace my gaze over an extremely fine painting. And, like an extremely fine painting, she began to make my heart beat faster. That was odd. I was never much attracted to random women, even before I dated Anna, even before Anna...well.

But this wasn't just my heart beating faster, my blood moving quicker through me. This was something else. A weightlessness, like being suspended in the air over the staircase again, the coolness of her palm against my skin a gravity that I seemed to suddenly spin around. When she gazed down into my eyes, she held me there as firmly as if her hands were snug against the small of my back, pressing me to her cool, lean body that wore the suit with such dignity and grace that I couldn't imagine her in anything else.

I was spellbound.

She said not a word, but her fingers left my wrist, grazing a little of the skin of my bare forearm for a heartbeat before her hand fell to her side. I shivered, holding my hand to my heart, then, as if I'd been bitten. We stood like that for a heartbeat, two, the woman's eyes never leaving mine as her chin lifted, as her jaw worked again, her full lips parting...

"Are you all right?" I shivered again. Her voice was dark, deep and throaty, as cool as her skin, as gentle as the touch of her fingertips along my arm. But as I gazed up at her, as I tried to calm my breathing, my heart, we blinked, she and I, together.

I knew, then.

I'd heard that voice before.

I'd seen this *face* before.

"Have we...met?" I stammered, eyes narrowed as I gazed up at her in wonder. We couldn't have. She shook her head and put it to the side as she looked down at me, as if I was a particularly difficult puzzle that needed solving. I would have remembered her, the curve of her jaw and lips, the dazzling blue of her eyes. I could never have forgotten her if I'd only seen her once. It would have been impossible.

I took a gulp of air and took a step back again, unthinking, and her hand was there, then, at my wrist again as she smoothly pulled me forward, toward her.

"The stairs," she said softly, apologetically. I'd taken a step closer to her this time, and there was hardly any space between us, even as I realized that my hand was at her waist, steadying myself against her. I took a step to the side, quickly, then, my cheeks burning.

"I'm sorry," I managed, swallowing. "And...thank you..." Her head was still to the side, but this time, her lips twitched as if she was trying to repress a smile.

"I've been meaning to remodel these steps. Not everyone knows how steep they truly are," she said, and her lips did turn up into a smile, then, making my heart beat a little faster. I took a great gulp of air as she held out her cool fingers to me, palm up.

"I am Kane Sullivan," she said easily, her tongue smoothing over the syllables as the smile vanished from her face. "You must be Rose Clyde," she said gently, the thrill of her voice, the deepness of it, the darkness of it, saying my name, the way her lips formed the words...I nodded my head up and down like a puppet, and I placed my hand in hers. Her fingers were *so cold*, as she shook my hand like a delicate thing, letting her palm slide regretfully over mine as she dropped my hand with a fluid grace I had to watch but still couldn't fully understand.

I was acting like an idiot. I'd seen

beautiful women before. But Kane wasn't beautiful. Not in that sense. She was...compelling. Her face, her gaze, her eyes, an impossibility of attraction. I felt, as I watched her, that buildings, trees, people would turn as she walked past them, unseeing things still, somehow, gazing at her.

I knew her, then.

The painting. The woman in the painting from last night, with the big, black cat, lounging and regal and triumphant and unspeakably bewitching. The naked woman, I realized, as my face began to redden, warming beneath her cool, silent gaze. She was the woman from the painting. But as I realized that, as we silently watched one another, I realized, too, that that would have been impossible. It had been a while since college, it was true, but I could still tell when a painting was a few hundred years old.

The woman in the painting could not possibly have been Kane Sullivan. And yet, it couldn't possibly have been anyone else.

"I'm...I'm sorry," I spluttered, realizing—again—how much of an idiot I must look to this incredibly attractive creature. Her lips twitched upward again, and her mouth stretched into a true smile this time, the warmth of it making the air around her seem less frozen.

"You're fine. It's not everyday that someone completely uproots their life and charts a course for places unknown," she said, turning on her heel and inclining her heard toward me. As she turned, I caught the scent of her. Jasmine, vanilla...spice. An intoxicating, cool scent that was warm at the same time. Unmistakable and deeply remarkable. Just like her. I stared up at her with wide eyes as she gestured gracefully with her arm for us to walk together, like she was a gentleman from the past century. True, she was wearing a sharp man's suit (that I was trying desperately not to stare at or trace the curves of it with my eyes—and failing), but there was something incredibly old fashioned about her. I kept thinking about that at that first meeting. Like she was from a different era, not the one of smart phones and the Internet and fast food french fries. No. The kind of era that had horse-drawn carriages, corsets and bustles and houses that contained parlors. We began to walk down the corridor together, in the opposite direction I had come, me sneaking surreptitious glances at her, her staring straight ahead.

The spell of the moment was broken, but a new spell was beginning to create itself, weaving around the two of us as we walked along the corridor. As she spoke, I stared half up at her, half down the hall stretching out in front of us. All of my actual attention, though, was on this woman.

Every bit of it. She was just like that.

So…compelling. She was a gravity that pulled me in, hook, line and sinker. I didn't know then how much of a gravity she had yet to become to me.

Follow along with the **Sullivan Vampires** saga by searching for "Sullivan Vampires" wherever you purchase your eBooks or print books or visit **http://bridgetessex.wordpress.com/about/**

Made in the USA
San Bernardino, CA
23 June 2016